THE MATTER OF

THE

DEPARTED

DIAMONDS

The Ultimate Locked Room Mystery

Steve Levi

Master Of The Impossible Crime

PUBLICATION
CONSULTANTS
WE BELIEVE IN THE POWER OF AUTHORS

PO Box 221974 Anchorage, Alaska 99522-1974
books@publicationconsultants.com, www.publicationconsultants.com

ISBN Number: 978-1-63747-116-6
eBook ISBN Number: 978-1-63747-117-3

Library of Congress Number: 2022943506

Manufactured in the United States of America

Some people have a skeleton with every bone crooked.

...Heinz Noonan

CHAPTER 1

Heinz Noonan, the "Bearded Holmes" of the Sandersonville Police Department, was happily ensconced in a particularly gripping cold case file when Harriett, the department office manager and common sense guru, slipped into his office, leaned over his shoulder and whispered in a low, malevolent tone, "Who knows what evil lurks ..."

"The Shadow," Noonan replied in a matching, deep, malevolent voice without missing a beat or looking up from the crime scene photos. "The Shadow knows what evil lurks in the hearts of men and I'm not old enough to remember the radio program so how can you?"

"I," Harriett said professorially as she straightened up, "have lived many lives. One of them was in the 1930s when I was an avid radio serialized drama listener." Her voice then became malevolent again. "I am the Dark Avenger." Thereafter, in a normal tone she said, "There's a call from a South Dakota State Trooper in the middle of nowhere. In a city called Micheaux. He's on Line Three. I had to look up Micheaux in South Dakota on Google Maps to make sure it wasn't a crank call. The call is real and South Dakota is. But I could not find Micheaux. But, I must say, if it is in South Dakota, it is NOT at the end of the earth."

Noonan looked up and said softly, "I know, but you can see it from there."

"Correct," snapped Harriet. And then she prestidigitated an airline ticket from behind her back. "And *His Majesty*, the Commissioner of Homeland Security, on the third floor says this is a matter of national security so you, *mein herr*, are booked on a flight to Sioux Falls from Virginia Beach in, oh," and she took a false look at the spot on her wrist where a wristwatch would have been if she did not have a cell phone which gave her the time 24/7, "three hours."

"I am *not* happy," snapped Noonan.

"Neither are six of the seven dwarfs." Harriett pointed to the phone. "Line Three. Sixty three diamonds have disappeared out of a locked vault."

"How'd that happen?"

"The *Shadow* knows!" Harriet said again in a low, sinister tone over her shoulder as she sidled out of Noonan's office.

Noonan picked up the phone, the landline, not the electronic tool of Satan his wife and the Sandersonville Commissioner of Homeland Security required him to have on his person at all times. At the same time, he picked up a notepad: "Noonan here."

"Captain Noonan?"

"No. Until there's a crime it's just Heinz. Who's this?"

"Moshe O'Reilly, I'm . . ."

"*Moshe O'Reilly*! How'd that happen?"

"Second marriage for both parents. I'm known as Walrus. As soon as you see me you'll know why."

"Let me guess, weight and a mustache like Yosemite Sam."

"Everything you'd expect of a walrus but the tusks. Heinz, I had to call you. Politics, unfortunately. My Commissioner of Homeland Security here in Sioux Falls, South Dakota somehow knows your Commissioner of Homeland Security and you can guess the rest of the story."

Noonan shook his head sadly. "Sure. The people of show expecting the people of sweat to make them look good in the press. From what I hear," Noonan said as he looked at the airline ticket in his hand, "I'm on my way to Sioux Falls."

"Initially, yes. Then by car to Micheaux."

"Why?"

"Sixty three diamonds have vanished out of a locked bank vault," he paused for a moment and then said. "My Commissioner thinks there's a Muslim connection."

CHAPTER 2

More than any other community in America, Sioux Falls, South Dakota, was a city built on credit.

In more ways than one.

Along with a hope and a prayer – with a heavy accent on the former.

The water falls for which Sioux Falls became named suggested promise for land speculators in the 1850s. So, in 1856, two competing land companies, the Dakota Land Company out of St. Paul, Minnesota, and the Western Town Company out of Dubuque, Iowa, both claimed 320 acres. Not the same 320 acres but close enough to make it worth their while to band together as a single unit. The greatest reason for the two companies working together were the hostile Indians who did not see these land companies as cozy neighbors. For that reason, the two companies combined their manpower – and womanpower as well – and constructed a crude fort for protection. Because the area had no trees, the fortress was made of sod and thus named "Fort Sod." The colony managed to make it through the winter of 1856 and the next spring the combined companies started a marketing arm and 'invited' settlers into the area.

At a per farm charge.

The boom lasted through a number of Indian *conflicts*, including the Dakota War of 1862, after which the site was abandoned. Thereafter every farm, ranch and structure was pillaged by the Indians and burned to the sod. Sod, as in the ground.

The site sat vacant for three years, until the end of the Civil War, when a military reservation was established on the former fort's foundation. The foundation, again, being sod. With soldiers in the new, re-named, Fort Dakota, many of the settlers who had fled the hostile Indians three years earlier, returned. This time the settlers were able to remain when the troops moved to another fort in 1869. Within four years so many settlers moved into the area there was a building boom and the population surged to a walloping 593! The town incorporated in 1876, just in time for the railroad boom of the 1880s. By then the city's population had increased by a factor of four. The city took a massive hit with a plague of grasshoppers and, thereafter, almost became a casualty of the Panic of 1893. The city survived thanks to the abundance of agricultural products which could be shipped east and a meatpacking plant located conveniently close to the railroad. During the Second World War, an airbase was established and a military communication school kept the economy going.

Then, true to its roots, the population of Sioux Falls took another jump in 1981 when the South Dakota Legislature loosened usury laws. This attracted Citibank to locate its credit card operation out of Sioux Falls. Other companies followed quickly and thereafter the area became a mini-Silicon Valley. But even by Heinz Noonan's standards, it was still a small city. Just over 180,00. "But it's still growing," Walrus told him.

Noonan had absolutely no idea what to expect when it came to Muslims. In South Dakota, Sandersonville or anywhere in the United States for that matter. To him, as well as most Americans, Islam were just another religion whose devotees were only visibly different because of their outfits. But religious dress was nothing new for Americans. Muslim women wore the *hijab*. Jewish men wore the *yarmulke* and the Sikh wore turbans. The Outer Banks of North Carolina saw a lot of all three religious orders because it was the summer playground of the East Coast. On the East Coast, one did not go "on a holiday," they went "on holiday" and that holiday lasted six weeks. A "vacation" on the West Coast was a week. At best. But the East Coast was different.

When you went "on holiday" it was for a month a half. During that month and a half, people of every race, religion and ethnic persuasion flooded the Outer Banks of North Carolina. The only thing all the tourists had in common was money. It took a fair chunk of change to take six weeks off for a vacation. Or holiday. For most Americans, those six weeks were called unemployment. But if you could afford to take six weeks off, you were doing well in life.

Noonan felt almost at home in Sioux Falls. Both Sandersonville and Sioux Falls were flat.

Very flat.

Yes, yes, there were some foothills in both geographic locales, but foothills were not mountains. The Black Hills were the closest mountains to Sioux Falls but they were a good 350 miles away. Noonan didn't care how far the mountains were from Sandersonville because the Atlantic Ocean beach was less than a mile from his office and a mile and a half from his home. When you had saltwater on your doorstep, why worry about how far away the nearest mountain range was?

The falls in Sioux Falls were impressive. All 100 feet of them. A bit impressive was the 18-foot high statue of David. Why a statue of David would be in the American heartland – and outside – puzzled Noonan. Then he learned the statue had been donated to the city along with the land for a park, Fawick Park, paid for by Thomas Fawick, a millionaire. What a surprise, Noonan thought. A millionaire giving money to a city to name a park after himself.

Noonan had no trouble picking Walrus out of the crowd at the Sioux Falls airport. Walrus, well, looked exactly like a walrus – with the exception of the tusks. He was massive, a good deal over six feet, probably 6' 7' or 6' 8", and was standing next to a man who might have topped five feet. If it wasn't for skull cap, the man standing next to Walrus would have disappeared in any crowd in America. This, Noonan surmised, must be the Muslim connection. *A Muslim with a skull cap?*, thought Noonan.

Noonan walked down the airport's portable staircase and shook Walrus' hand. "Let me guess, you're Walrus."

"Tough to tell, right?" Walrus laughed. "This is Ambrose Brody. He's with Brody and Sons. He's one of the 'sons,' by the way. Old Man Brody is gone and the other sons are somewhere in the Middle East selling diamonds."

"Is that good or bad?" Noonan asked.

Brody smiled. When he spoke, his English was perfect. "Good. One brother is the sales arm of Brody and Sons in the Middle East and the other is our investment specialist. None of us are radicals, we're businessmen." He pointed at Walrus, "Unlike the belief of the Sioux Falls Commissioner of Homeland Security, we are not a security risk."

"We live in strange times," Noonan said. "Speaking for all reasonable Americans, let me apologize for the attitude of too many Americans, particularly those in public office."

"Or running for public office," Walrus put in.

Brody smiled and kind of nodded his head. Then Walrus took Noonan's boarding pass and left to get the luggage. This gave Noonan a chance to talk with Brody one-on-one.

"That's an odd briefcase, Captain." Brody said as he pointed at Noonan's briefcase,

"Heinz. I'm Heinz until there's a crime."

"Fine with me. I'm Ambrose. And just in case you are wondering, yes, I am a Muslim and I am from the Middle East. I come from a large extended family that stretches from the United Arab Emirates to London. I grew up in Saudi Arabia. My father chose to be in the precious stones trade as a young man. He was not interested in moving money from bank to bank. He knew there was too much chicanery involved in cash. He preferred precious stones. They have a provenance. Do you know what a provenance is?"

Noonan nodded. "Paperwork which lists who bought the property from whom, when and for how much."

"Very good. I'm pleased to see a man from the Outer Banks of North Carolina knows the intricate realities of making sure art and relics are authentic when they are sold as authentic."

Noonan kind of nodded. "Everything of value has a provenance. Most of the *valuable* items I have had to deal with call it a title."

Brody laughed. "Well said." He pointed at Noonan's briefcase again. "It's odd. I've never seen one like it before. Why is it vertical rather than horizontal?"

Noonan gave the briefcase a slight lift. "This was my father's briefcase," He gave it a shake. "You are correct. Most briefcases are horizontal, so legal briefs, which are usually 8 ½ by 14 inches, can fit in with the 14-inch folders flush along the bottom. My father was injured during the Second World War and had a badly disfigured right leg. It was rock solid with its patella stick out the back. It made carrying a traditional briefcase difficult. It affected his balance when he walked. So he had a briefcase specially made. This one, as a matter of fact. It's 8 ½ inches along the bottom and 14 inches high. He is long gone and I use his briefcase for good luck."

"You'll need it in this case," Walrus cut in and he came back with Noonan's suitcase. "We need a Holmes for this case."

"I've been lucky," Noonan said.

"We can use all the luck we can get on this case," Walrus said. He pointed toward a car on the runway with the suitcase indicating that was the way they were going to be leaving the landings strip. As Walrus walked toward his unmarked, he was so large Noonan's suitcase appeared more like a briefcase than luggage.

The trip across Sioux Falls was just long enough to be boring. Walrus pointed out some of the sights, which were of interest to Noonan but not to Brody. "I've lived here for six years," he told Noonan. "I've seen it all. The town's not that large."

"I have to ask," Noonan said. "Since the reason I am here is because we've got some Commissioners of Homeland Security who are fearful of Muslims, do you live here?"

"Actually," Brody said. "I do. I have an office here. I'm like a lot of people in business here. I came for a job expecting to spend six weeks. Six years later, I'm still here."

"Why here?" Noonan asked as he pointed to the flatlands.

"Brody and Sons specialize in precious stones. We, rather I, picked up loose stones in Europe and America and then the company, my brothers and their families, sell them in the Middle East. In America, there are, generally speaking, three ways of getting stones. One is buying imports from Africa which is now illegal. I don't have a problem with that. Blacks in Africa are treated a lot worse than blacks here in the United States. And if you want to know, I am a citizen of the United States. Dual, actually. Have been for a long time. I married my wife, an American, while I was in Italy on assignment. She was working for an American company as an economist. We saw how women were treated in Catholic countries and we're not going to have our daughters be treated that way."

"You have children?"

"Three daughters. Daughters are always a handful. One is an MD, another is the wife of a businessman and the third, well, she's still finding herself in San Francisco. In the theater." Brody looked at Noonan over a shoulder. "I'm telling you these things so you don't think I'm some sheik of the Araby. There are a lot of myths about Arabs running around in America."

"There are a lot of myths about Americans running around in America," Noonan said with a smile. "As fathers, we're in the same boat, brother. I've got twins. One is a lawyer in Seattle and the other is in Boston and I am never sure what it is he is doing except that it's legal."

Both men laughed

"Back to diamonds, Heinz," Brody shook his head sadly. "It is a rugged business. The reason we have done so well is we, or rather I, am good at finding heirlooms. If I were to buy diamonds on the open market, say, in New York or Philadelphia or Atlanta, any big city, I'd be forced to pay top dollar. The market price. There's profit there but not as much as the heirlooms."

"What do you mean by heirlooms?"

"By heirlooms, I mean diamonds, sapphires, rubies, what you call precious stones, that are in rings, pendants and lapel pins someone gave someone else years ago. Like your great grandmother's wedding ring. That kind of a thing. It was valuable then and passed down, generation after generation, because it is a family relic. But six generations later, no one is really sure why the ring or pendant was special. So they want to sell it. Someone in Sioux Falls, for instance, inherits jewelry from a maiden aunt. Say, a pinky ring. It's gold with a diamond inset. The jewelry might have been special to the maiden aunt but not to the nephew or cousin who inherited the item. So the pinky ring is sold to a jeweler. The jeweler extracts the precious stone from the pinky ring and sells the gold and diamond separately. A free stone requires a GemPrint before it sold. Do you know what that is?"

Noonan smiled. "Fingerprint, so to speak. But for a diamond."

"Correct," Brody said. "If you are a jeweler, you can buy whatever gems you want. But if you buy a stolen gem, the police will confiscate the item. The way to avoid buying stolen property is to see if the item you want to buy has a GemPrint. Yes, like a fingerprint. The results are on the internet, just a finger-click away. Before any jeweler buys a gem, he checks the GemPrint. If it is stolen merchandise, he turns it over to the police. If it is not on some list of stolen objects, the jeweler is sure the gem is good enough to sell on its own or use in a piece of jewelry."

Brody continued. "When it comes to heirloom jewelry, every stone that is bought has to be checked against the GemPrint database. So the local jeweler who has just extracted the diamond from that pinky ring, usually won't pay for the diamond until the word comes back that the gem has not been stolen and cleverly put in an old pinky ring gold body to fool a jeweler. That takes time and money. So, in terms of dollars and cents, it's cheaper, and more profitable for the heirloom owner to sell the stone to someone else who is willing to take the chance the gem might have been stolen."

"That would be you." Noonan smiled.

"That would be me, yes. But not in this case. In most cases, and not this one, I buy the stone and spend the time and money to see if a piece I have bought has a GemPrint and was not stolen property. And if there is no GemPrint, I get one made for that piece of jewelry. I'm not dealing in bulk so it's worth my time. There are lots of people like me in the San Franciscos, Philadelphias and Atlantas but in the Midwest, not so much. Sioux Falls turned out to be a good location because it is kind of a Silicon Valley in the Midwest. A lot of people come here to work in the financial corporations. They are on their way up in the corporate world and if the heirloom mean nothing to them, the sell the items locally. I end up with the gems and the jewelers sell the gold locally. In this case, I am brokering the diamonds. I don't have the money to buy the diamonds in this big of a lot."

"So there's a lot of business in gems here?"

"In the Midwest, not enough for a large company. But for someone who is willing travel for a few diamonds here and a few sapphires there, yes. Which is why a one-person operation like me can be successful."

"So you get the GemPrint for every stone?"

"It's not hard, but it is time consuming. That's why the larger jewelers don't want to spend the time doing it. Besides, if the gem turns out to be stolen, they're out what they paid for the stone."

"How many stones that do not have a GemPrint do you see in a year?"

"A few. Not many. Don't forget, I deal in stones in the onesies and twosies. That's the only way I can make a profit. I buy the gems here, check to make sure they are legal, then send them to my brothers in Saudi Arabia. It has been quite profitable here in the Midwest. That's why I'm still living here."

Noonan kind of looked around. Brody caught the drift.

"I know what you are thinking, Heinz. You have that cop look. That's OK. I don't have a problem setting you at ease. After all, you're here to find the 63 diamonds that disappeared."

Noonan was a bit surprised. "What do you mean by the 'cop look?'"

Brody smiled. "Cops think in terms of custody. When something is stolen, they start with who owned what and who owned it before and so on. A train of custody. What you are thinking is 'what is the chain of custody of any one of the raw stones I buy and could some of them disappear into my pocket.'"

"Well, that's not exactly...."

Brody smiled. "Not a problem, Heinz. I'm above board. It is not worth my time to shave a little profit on the side. What goes around comes around. Jewelers who take shortcuts usually get caught. When I get a stone, I send it registered to a firm that does the GemPrinting. They send it back to me with the GemPrint. I keep the stones until I get a package of twenty and then I send them to my brother overseas.

There is a paper trail for every stone and remember, in the United States, there is the IRS. You do not want to run afoul of the IRS."

"Never had the pleasure," Noonan said with a smirk. "Tell me about the 63 diamonds that disappeared."

"That's an odd one, Heinz. Even for me. It started with an eccentric multimillionaire, possibly a billionaire. His name was Kankan Musa. It was originally James Clarkson. He was black, the great-great-grandson of a buffalo soldier. In the 1970s, when Black Nationalism was the rage, he changed his name to Kankan Musa. Well-educated, he made a killing in real estate and on the stock market. A very smart man, he spread his money around and quadrupled his wealth in a decade and doubled it decade after decade. He saw a future in historical items, particularly those with a connection to black history."

Brody leaned back and stretched before he went on. "Rather than live here in Sioux Falls, he founded his own town, so to speak. He bought an abandoned community sixty miles down the road from here, Combine. That was its name when it was incorporated in the 1930s. Renamed it Micheaux after the black film producer."

Noonan was surprised. "He bought a *city*?"

Brody smiled. "An *abandoned* city. It was abandoned in the 1950s or 1960s. It was just in the farmland deteriorating when he bought it. Got it on a bank foreclosure."

"Why buy an abandoned city?"

Brody laughed. "I'm sure everyone in Sioux Falls thought the same thing at the time. There wasn't a dime in value there. But he bought it anyway and turned it into a mini-Silicon Valley. What he knew then we know now, particularly with the impact of COVID-19, is where you work is not necessarily in some office building. You can work from home. And now, with the expansion of the internet and," Brody looked up at the sky and pointed, "it won't be long before we can beam solar power down from above. He saw that coming."

Noonan shook his head. "That would have been quite a while in the future when he bought the abandoned city."

"Not if you are a visionary, Heinz. Kankan Musa did well with the community. He put in solar power, restored the power grid, upgraded the water and sewer facility, began producing one of a kind art objects for online sales, made it profitable for family farmers to come back to the land and grow crops that took a lot of effort but had a niche in the market. Organics. Along with some egg farms, grass-fed beef and pork and then he expanded into the remote hunting and fishing industries. Like I said, he was well ahead of his time. Everything he touched was profitable. He started with an abandoned town with dilapidated buildings that now has more than 100 full-time residents and I don't know how many folks working out of their homes."

Noonan smiled. "I love dreamers. What's his connection to the diamonds?"

"Another brilliant move. He read the future like a book. He realized that while precious stones have a relatively stable price, precious metals do not. That's one of the oddity of the precious stone markets. That market does not follow the Law of Supply and Demand. In most cases, when someone buys a stone, a diamond or sapphire, they keep it. Expect to put in jewelry at some time. Jewelry is the same way. People do not look at the diamonds and sapphires in grandma's broach as money. They see grandma's broach as a piece of family history. It gets passed down generation after generation. It's special. It does not get sold. Afterall, it's snapshot of the past. The family's past."

Brody paused before he continued. "Gold is different. It does not have a personality like a broach or a pinkie ring. If someone has an ounce of gold or a pound of silver, they are not adverse to selling it. When they make the decision to sell the metal, they usually open the newspaper and look at the price of gold or silver on that day. They are not actually looking to see what the value of gold is that day. They are looking to see if the price is going up or down. The gold is not a heirloom, it is a liquid investment. When the price is right, they sell."

Noonan stalled for a moment while he dug for a notebook. "Just a second. I need to write this down." After he had his notebook opened, he indicated for Brody to go on.

Brody continued. "Kankan guessed – and correctly as it turned out – over the long run, the price of gold would go up. It always has. At some times rather rapidly. For investment purposes, gold has been on a steady rise. He figured to beat the system by buying heirloom jewelry. It offered a long term investment bonanza. He could buy a ring, for instance, and have two investments at the same time: the stones and the metal. He had quite a stash."

"Why did he suddenly decide to sell?"

"Apparently he felt it was the right time to liquidate the heirlooms. He started the dismantling of the heirlooms and then he got cancer. About three years ago. It's taken that long for the gold and precious stones to get through probate. You see," Brody looked at Noonan with a wink and a grin, "everyone is fighting for a cut of the pie."

"Must have been one heck of a pie," Noonan said.

"Massive," Brody shook his head. "Kankan Musa lived modestly. Was a visionary and visionaries are not to be hindered by the here and now. His relatives do not have, shall we say, quite the same vision."

"Let me guess," Noonan said shaking his head sadly. "They want to butcher his empire."

"Way of the world, Heinz. The way of the world."

"OK," Noonan said. "The way of the world is also cash. So, are the diamonds. What are we talking about for value?"

"Complicated questions, Heinz. Some basics are necessary for the answer. The value of a diamond is based on four or five factors. Generally speaking it is the shape of the diamond, the carat size, color, clarity and cut. An excellent diamond sells for more than a poorly cut one. I do not know where Kankan got his background in gems but he knew what he was buying. He bought the best. At least that's what he ended up with. In terms of dollars, because that's what you want, right?"

"Correct," Noonan said as he waited with pen in hand over a notebook page.

"About $2 million. In the United States. In the Middle East where the market is tighter and the money looser, twice that. That being said, I'd say there are three or four stones that would fetch upwards of $100,000 for their color, clarity, cut and carat size. But that's just a guess."

Noonan nodded his head as he wrote. "Clearly worth someone's time to steal."

"Apparently," replied Brody.

CHAPTER 3

Walrus did not bother to take Noonan and Brody to his office. He drove directly to the Micheaux Transport and Delivery armored car facility. "No use going to my office," Walrus said, "We're going to go directly to one of the scenes of the crime." He parked in front of the armored car company and the three of them walked through the security screening at the main door. Walrus gave up his pistol. Noonan breezed right on through.

"No gun?" Walrus asked with curiosity.

"Never needed one," Noonan replied.

The three of them were led downstairs to a lunch room next to the vault. After they sat down, Noonan pulled a notebook from his briefcase. "OK, let's take this a step at a time." He looked at Brody, "Start from the beginning."

Brody pulled a sheaf of papers from the briefcase he had been carrying. He handed the papers to Noonan.

"These are the contract papers, Heinz. In a nutshell, in the beginning, Kankan Musa, who I told you about on our way in, collected quite a few pieces of heirloom jewelry. Where he got them I do not know. But it didn't matter. What did matter was the paperwork, the provenances. The term *provenance* is actually the specific term for ownership records of high end artwork. No auction house is going to sell a Picasso without a provenance and every one is checked thoroughly. But when it comes to heirloom jewelry, the term provenance does not fit. Bill of sale does. Before I would agree to broker the stones I needed to look over his records. He got all of the pieces legally and recorded the sales. But this was over a 20 or 30-year time span. He got sick about 12 years ago so there were no purchases over those years."

Brody pointed at the paperwork he had handed Noonan. "I hate to bore you with details but ..."

Noonan smiled. "It's the details that make all the difference in solving a crime. Bore me."

Brody smiled. "Even my wife doesn't want to know the details. OK, the process I use is simple. I verify as much as I can the actual acquisition of the heirloom. In most cases, there is no paperwork. Some grandfather – or was it a great grandparent – back in days after the Civil War bought his bride a diamond pendant and it has been in the family ever since. Now the family wants to sell it. There is no paperwork. Or if there was, it's very old or generic. By generic, I mean, the item was one of 100 that was made and every one of the 100 pendants got the same proof of authenticity. If that. It would be the kind of document anyone could reproduce on a computer."

"But in the case of Kankan Musa," Noonan guessed. "What you had were bills of sale, so to speak. Like, Joe and Mary Jones agree to sell this ring with the diamond and sapphire to Kankan Musa for $325."

"Correct. Almost. Some of the items were sold to James Clarkson, Kankan's name before he became Kankan."

"So, he bought 63 items and the diamonds are missing."

"Actually, no. There were a total of 153 precious stones extracted from the heirloom jewelry. Only the diamonds are missing. 63 of them. The rest of the stones are not missing. Actually, I do not know how many individual heirloom pieces there were originally because I only examined the stones. If a pendant had three stones, that would reduce the overall number of pieces of jewelry. But that's not the point. Currently there are 63 diamonds missing. That's the number that's important."

Noonan was scribbling away. "So Kankan bought, say, a gold ring with a diamond and then put it in a vault for safekeeping?"

"I don't know where he kept the jewelry but it was organized. I know that from the paperwork. His death was long and lingering but at no point in his downward journey did he sign any documents as to who should inherit which stones. He did not have any natural children but took in about a dozen and raised them as his children. None were adopted on paper. The only paperwork regarding the inheritance of the heirloom jewelry was a sort-of holographic will from ten years before his death. I have been told, not that it makes any difference to me because I am only interested in brokering the stones, he did not scatter any of his holdings to specific individuals. That's yet to be done. The heirloom jewelry is not even a modest part of the wealth to be transferred to whomever."

"So how was the heirloom jewelry to be passed along?"

"I'm getting to that. It's a short but twisted story."

"Note the look of surprise on my face," Noonan said as he pointed his face. "A lot of wealth to be divided among people who want it all. How unique!"

Brody chuckled. "You got it. And I have to tell you because it will illustrate how awkward the ownership of the diamonds was. And is. Generally speaking, and again, I had to piece this together from conversations with Kankan over a four-year period, his estate was supposed to be divided among the children he had raised. Maybe. In addition to having no Last Will and Testament giving specific people specific items of property, there was the problem of finding those who might inherit something. Some of them had died. Some had left South Dakota for parts unknown. Others had blended families. Others had estranged children adopted by the new wife or husband. Others were dead but there were children who claimed to be real, adopted or taken in by someone who might inherit. Some were Democrats, others were Republicans, some were black, others with white or Native or whatever. It is not like Kankan had one big happy family that got together every Labor Day."

"Sounds like a typical American family," Noonan said. "And when money was dropped on the table, the catfighting started."

Now Walrus cut in. "Yup. Sometimes the fighting was fierce. Sioux Falls was the nearest community with a police force so that left law and order in Micheaux to the State Troopers. That meant me. I'm the one who got the calls. Eventually I was put in charge of the complaints in Micheaux. I guess I spend about three days a month in Micheaux or the surrounding area. Everything from drunk and disorderly, property damage, DV, property disputes. Nothing big but a lot of little stuff."

Noonan looked at Walrus oddly. "Why no police in Micheaux? It wasn't big enough?"

"Oh, it was big enough," Walrus said. "Kankan Musa didn't trust the city cops. Probably had a problem with the police as a youngster. The city is still officially Combine. It has not been legally renamed. Kankan talked about naming it Micheaux. Officially, that is. Micheaux, South Dakota. But he either never had the time to do it or the person who was supposed to do it never did. We'll talk about him in a bit. A real piece of work. Attucks Musa."

"Relative?" asked Noonan.

"Nephew by birth, adopted by Kankan," Brody said. Then Brody looked around, as if to see who might be listening. When Brody looked at Walrus, Walrus kind of shook his head sadly and gave an indication Brody should go on.

"Heinz, I was educated in Europe. So I use a lot of European expressions that have no meaning in the United States. Are you familiar with the term 'knight and barrow pig?'"

"No," Noonan said with a laugh. "But I like it."

Brody continued. "A knight and barrow pig is someone who has no social skills at all. He is a social climber with no money. Kind of yes man who hangs around the king."

"A myrmidon, right?"

"Worse. A myrmidon is more of a hitman on payroll, to so speak. Like a Mafia mobster. He is not in charge. He simply takes orders without considering the consequences to himself or the boss. A knight and barrow pig is someone who is worming his way to fortune by sucking up to the king. The king makes him a knight because the king is tired of being pestered by that person to make him a knight."

"Let me guess," Noonan said. "When he becomes the knight he is insufferable."

"That," Brody said sadly, "Is only a part of the story." Now that he is a knight he keeps everyone else away from the king, does things in the king's name the king may or may not want done, represents the king whether the king wants it done or not.

"I know the kind."

"In this case, it's worse. As Kankan's health declined, this individual took over more and more of the duties Kankan had done when he was healthy. At the end of the day, so to speak, Attucks was running the whole show. From the nuts-and-bolts of the sewage utility operation to distributing property according to what he said Kankan wanted him to do and," Brody pointed at the sheaf of papers in Noonan's hand, "the sale of the heirloom jewelry."

"So he runs the show?"

Brody nodded. "The whole show. Over the years he squeezed out everyone who was close to Kankan. He started out as the go-to-guy and now he runs the show."

"Honest?"

Brody wobbled his head, not a 'yes' or a 'no.' "I have no way of knowing. While I was dealing with Kankan when Kankan was alive, Attucks followed the instructions. Sucking up, yes. But then again, there was no one else left to do the work. I didn't deal with Attucks on any other issues. Just the gems. So, is he honest? I don't know. But he does know the city and its workings from the ground up. He's the man who runs Micheaux."

Noonan looked at Walrus. "Do you have anything to add?"

"Not really. When I am in Micheaux, he's the man I deal with. No one else. He tells me what's wrong and I fix it. He is not a pleasant person to deal with. He's out of the 1960s with the attitude of 'I am a black man and I am proud to be a black man' even though no one cares. But he manages the nuts-and-bolts of the city."

"Did Attucks keep Micheaux from getting a police force?" Noonan pointedly looked at Walrus.

"Not the way you mean it," Walrus replied. "It has a community patrol but no one carries a gun. No reason to. You did not need money in Micheaux. It was all debit or credit cards. If you wanted cash in large amounts, you have to come to Sioux Falls. If you want to buy something big, like a car, all the paperwork goes through Sioux Falls banks."

"That seems a bit unusual," Noonan commented.

"Not really," Walrus said. "You have to understand the actual population of those who live in Micheaux year-round is a fewer more than 100. They shop for the little stuff in the local stores but the bulk of the shopping is in Sioux Falls. There are about another 200 people who work at their home in Sioux Falls for the high-tech operations headquartered out of Micheaux. But they rarely go to Micheaux. Zoom and all. So it makes sense for everyone to use credit and debit cards locally."

"Is there a bank in Micheaux?" Noonan asked.

Walrus laughed. "Yes, but not the way you mean it."

"How do I mean it?" Noonan asked.

Walrus leaned back his chair and the wood gave a squeak. Walrus righted himself. "What you mean by a bank is a building where you can go in and cash a check or open a safety deposit box. In that sense, no Micheaux does not have that kind of a bank. But it does have a vault for records, the heirlooms, backup digital copies for the computers and other business items. The actual structure was an old, refrigerated building. It was upgraded to a secure vault and has all of the modern security devices like cameras, temperature control, time locks."

"But no money," Noonan cut it.

"No money, that's right." Walrus then added, "There are some lockboxes for locals but no big ones. Like I said, it's primarily a paper and digital holding vault."

"That's where the heirlooms were kept?"

Now Brody re-entered the conversation. "That I, we, do not know. But it is where the gems from the heirlooms ended up. Or, it is where the gems were extracted from the heirloom jewelry. As far as I know, the gold and silver bodies of the jewelry have long since been melted down and sold. There have been no complaints of the authenticity or value of the gold and silver. Just the diamonds."

"Just the diamonds," Noonan said with a strange look on his face. "None of the other stones are missing?"

"Odd, I know." Brody broke in. "Yes. The extraction involved all types of precious stones. But only the diamonds are missing."

"You said *missing*," Noonan said, accenting the word *missing*.

"Correct," Walrus chimed in. "The only items *missing* are the diamonds" He also accentuated the word *missing*. "63 of them. When I was called on the case I was told to track all of the gems. I don't know rubies and sapphires from hog jowls, but the jewelers who got the shipment of precious stones in Omaha, confirmed the precious stones that were *not* diamonds were authentic and had been received, all of them, in their facility. But they did not look at the diamonds. They were not supposed to. They opened the cabinet with the gems and only took out the drawers for the precious gems that were not diamonds. They did not open the other drawer. Then the drawer with the diamonds went back into the armored car and on to Kansas City, Missouri and the GemPrint facility."

"Did the cabinet go with the diamonds."

"Yup," Walrus said. "The cabinet went too. The facility in Omaha only took the drawers with the precious stones that were not diamonds. They relocked the cabinet and it was put back in the armored car. The cabinet went on to Kansas City with no stops along the way."

"And only the diamonds were missing?" Noonan asked.

"Yup."

"*Missing*," Noonan said again. "As in stolen?"

"That, oh 'Bearded Holmes' of the Outer Banks of North Carolina, is why you are here in Sioux Fall, South Dakota, the Mount Rushmore State."

CHAPTER 4

It took an hour for Walrus and Brody to flesh out the details of the *missing* diamonds. They kept using the term *missing* with an accent which indicated to Noonan there was something else involved beyond the diamonds. When in doubt, Noonan knew, 'follow the money.'

Then he hit the nail on the head.

"Well," Noonan said as he looked over his notes. "At this moment there is no robbery, just *missing*." He accented the word as Walrus and Brody had been doing. "To me, the cop, *missing* is substantially different than *stolen*. There is no legal definition of *missing*."

Brody responded quickly, "That, Heinz, is the secondary problem here. Right now, because there is a difference between *missing* and *stolen*, the entire case is in limbo. The diamonds are insured for loss, theft and destruction, but not *missing*. So we have a conundrum. We do not have the diamonds. They were not stolen, damaged or destroyed so there is no insurance coverage. Everyone is under suspicion because no one knows how the diamonds disappeared."

Noonan did a long mmm and then said. "Let me guess, the insurance company does not want you to use the term stolen because then it has to pay for the loss. When will the diamonds be considered *stolen*?"

Walrus and Brody looked at each other. Finally, Brody said, "It really doesn't matter whether the term is *missing* or *stolen*, some insurance company is going to eventually pay. It just depends on which one. The diamonds were insured for transit. The diamonds are covered under the insurance for the bank. The diamonds are covered if they disappear," he made motions with his hands to indicate 'poof and gone,' "in the armored car. There is lots of coverage."

Walrus added. "Right now, it's a catfight with the insurance companies as to which one is going to pay. I'm not in the insurance business but my bet is that, at the end of the day, missing or stolen, the insurance companies will split the loss. That's actually good news for them. It gives them an excuse to raise rates. So, for me, in the law enforcement business, the diamonds are missing. For him," he pointed at Ambrose Brody, "they are just misplaced merchandise. But for you," now he pointed at Noonan, "they are stolen because you are here and do not have a supervisor breathing down your neck with an open dictionary."

Noonan gave a grimace and looked over his notes. "OK, let me go over this slowly. Let me tell you two what happened and you tell me when I go wrong."

Walrus looked at Brody who nodded his head.

"You," Noonan pointed at Brody, "were contacted to be the distributor of the precious stones. You are not the buyer, just the distributor."

"Correct," Brody said. "All of the precious stones. Not just the diamonds. All the stones that came out of the heirlooms. No bodies. That is, none of the gold and silver surrounding the gemstones."

Noonan continued. "Those precious stones included more than just diamonds. There were also sapphires, rubies and emeralds."

"Correct," said Brody.

Noonan looked at Brody. "Did you actually do the removal of the precious stones from the heirlooms?"

"No. The extraction had already been done. Attucks had done it over time. When I got to the Micheaux vault, the stones were on a table for me examine."

"Were the heirloom gold and silver bodies and whatever else still in the vault?"

"Not as far as I know. I mean, I didn't ask to see them. There was no reason to see them because I had only been contracted to deal with the gemstones. I am just the distributor. I was to coordinate the sale of the precious stones. The way it was to work, financially, was that I would borrow money for a down payment on all the stones. For insurance purposes."

Brody took a breath. "I spent several days in the Micheaux Bank vault where I examined all 153 stones. Each stone was placed in a separate envelope, a gemstone enveloped. The gemstone envelopes were placed in three drawers, one for the diamonds and two for the other stones. The cabinet was locked and the cabinet was loaded into an armored car. The cabinet was then sent by armored car to a jewelry clearing house in Omaha, Nebraska, where the diamonds would be separated from the other gemstones. The GemPrint was only for the diamonds. Those stones which were not diamonds were removed in Omaha. The diamonds were sent on to the GemPrint facility in Kansas City."

Noonan was writing furiously. Brody continued. "Keeping the explanation as simple as possible, I would than catalog the stones by size and purity. I would send the catalog to my brother in Riyadh. In Saudi Arabia. He would distribute the catalog and coordinate any sales. When there was a sale of a specific stone, I would package the stone and send it."

"By mail?"

"Usually not. I don't want to discuss the ways the stones are sent to Riyadh. But the route is secure. We've never had a stolen gem. Or a missing one, for that matter."

"OK," Noonan said as he looked at his notes. "So in the vault in Micheaux you sat at a table and went through 63 diamonds."

Brody added, "The 63 stones were just the diamonds. Total precious stones were 157. There were about a dozen more that were unsalable."

"Unsalable?"

"Badly chipped, zirconia or cut glass. I can only sell high-quality stones."

"So you went over the 157 precious stones. One at a time?"

"One at a time."

"How would you know if any of the stones you were examining had been stolen?"

"I would not. That's why you get a GemPrint. That's why the diamonds, not the other precious stones, were being sent to a GemPrint facility. The other precious stones, well, I had to depend on the paperwork for the purchase of the heirloom."

"And none of the other precious stones are missing."

"Correct, only the 63 diamonds."

"And you had no way of knowing if any of those diamonds were stolen property?"

"Correct again. I would not know if any stones were stolen property until the GemPrints came back on the diamonds. In the vault in Micheaux, all I knew was that I had to examine 157 precious stones for their salability. Like I said before, about a dozen did not make the cut. Sixty-three diamonds and 94 precious stones did."

"And only the diamonds are missing?"

"Correct."

"And there is no way of knowing if any of the missing stones were GemPrinted."

"Correct again. Rarely do heirloom diamonds get GemPrinted. The stones were inserted years ago. There was no GemPrint at that time. People who own heirlooms wear them and give them to descendants. There was no way to Gemprint in those days and even if there had been, there was no reason to GemPrint those stones. They were going into jewelry. That's why the stones are so salable once stolen."

"Can you sell GemPrinted diamonds?"

"If you mean on the open market, yes. If you mean like in a pawn shop, it is unlikely. In most of the world, every diamond that shows up for sale is checked for its GemPrint. If it has not been GemPrinted before, it is then. The only place you could sell stolen diamonds with a GemPrint is in the Far East where some buyers are not picky about where the stones came from. Even if the GemPrinted diamonds are discovered in, say, China, there is little you can do to get the gem back."

"But these heirloom diamonds have not been optically fingerprinted."

"Yes. So if they got stolen or went *missing*," Brody emphasized the word *missing* again. "They could be sold on the open market with no one the wiser."

"And none of the other precious stones had been GemPrinted or were being sent to be GemPrinted."

"As far as I knew, and know, none of the stones, diamonds or other precious gems, have been GemPrinted. Only the diamonds were being sent on to be GemPrinted."

"And none of the other precious stones are missing."

"Correct again."

"When you got to the vault, were all the diamonds in a pile and you went through them one after the other?"

"No. All of the precious stones, diamonds included, were in small envelopes with indications of which heirloom the stone had come from. My job was to roll each stone out of its envelope, verify it was a salable stone and then initial the envelope."

"Why initial the envelope?"

"Just to make sure I wasn't looking at the same stone twice. If a piece of jewelry had, say, three diamonds and two sapphires, there would be five envelopes. I wanted to make sure I looked at all five stones. All the envelopes look the same. Just the inked wording was different."

"So you examined all the precious stones?"

"Yes."

"And you put your initials on each envelope you examined."

"Yes."

"Then you put each diamond back in the envelope it came in."

"I put each precious stone back in the envelope it came in."

"Then what did you do with the envelopes?"

"There were three drawers. Removable drawers. Drawers from a vertical, traditional precious stone retainer cabinet. I put the diamonds in the envelopes in one drawer and then the other precious stones in two other drawers."

"Why did you separate the diamonds?"

"They were going to be sent to the GemPrint facility in Kansas City. The other precious stones were going to Omaha."

"I can understand that," Noonan said. "I have to keep track of the difference in my notes."

"Did the precious stones make it Omaha?"

"Yes. Rather, I was not informed any were missing. The armored car out of Micheaux went straight to Omaha, a 200-mile trip, a little over four hours. Omaha was the first stop. As far as I know, again, all of the stones not diamonds made it to Omaha."

"But none of the diamonds made the GemPrint facility in Kansas City?"

"Correct."

"How long did you spend examining the precious stones and putting them back in the envelopes?"

"In Micheaux?"

"Here."

"I didn't examine any stones here or in Omaha. The stones went through Sioux Falls on their way to Omaha. That's where the stones were separated. The rubies and sapphires stayed in Omaha. The diamonds went on to Kansas City. I only have a contract to distribute the diamonds. I examined the rubies and sapphires as a courtesy."

"How long did you spend examining all of the stones in Micheaux?"

"Three days. Not straight. A few hours one day, an hour or so the next day and then about six hours the day before the gems were to be sent on to Omaha and Kansas City."

"Where were you at the time of the transfer of the gems and diamonds into the armored car?"

"In the vault. I did a last-minute check to make sure the diamonds had not vanished overnight. Strange things can happen to precious gems, you know."

Noonan raised his eyebrows, "So I have been told." Noonan looked at his notes. "How long were you in the vault examining stones before they went into the armored car?"

"Maybe five minutes. It was just a cursory look. I looked in some envelopes, squeezed some others. At that time the diamonds were in their envelopes."

"You are sure."

"I looked and squeezed about a dozen envelopes, half of them diamonds. There were no empty envelopes. If all 63 diamonds had been missing, I would have known it instantly. None of the envelopes I squeezed were empty."

"Then the envelopes you had just squeezed were locked in a drawer."

"Yes. There were three drawers, two for rubies and sapphires and one for diamonds. I watched as all three drawers went into the cabinet."

"Then the cabinet door was locked."

"Yes. Attucks Musa locked it. He yelled something like 'OK' or "Come get it.' Three people, two women and a man, came into the vault. They were all wearing uniforms for Micheaux Transport and Delivery. They loaded the cabinet on a flat car and pulled it out of the vault."

"You followed them?"

"All the way to the armored car. And, yes, I looked inside the back of the armored car to make sure there was not another cabinet of the same make and model which could haeve been used to do a bait and switch."

"There wasn't one."

"Nope. Then a man and woman got in the back and the other woman locked the back door. She got in the driver's seat and away the armored car went."

"No one was following?"

"Not at five in the morning. Or, if they were, they did have their lights on. It wasn't dark, as in pitch black, but it was predawn. I saw no one following the armored car, or, for that matter, on the streets of Micheaux."

"Who else was there when the precious stones were loaded?"

"Well, there was a security guard outside the vault. The security guard never came into the vault. Attucks popped the vault door open, entered and then unlocked the cabinet. Then he pulled out the three drawers and set them on the table where I had been examining the stones the previous three days. Then he left the vault and stood in the hallway as I examined the stones. When I had finished examining the stones for shipment, he came back into the vault. He replaced the three drawers into the cabinet and then locked the cabinet. Specifically for your question, inside the vault, other than me and the armored car people, there was only one person: Attucks Musa. But he did not go into the vault until after I had examined the stones for shipment. Then he locked the door behind us, me and the armored car people, after we left."

"He loaded the drawers, correct. Not you?"

"He loaded the three drawers and locked the cabinet."

"OK. Then what happened?"

"For me, nothing. I came back here to Sioux Falls. For the moment, my job was done. After the diamonds had been GemPrinted, I would make the arrangement for sale and transport.. The load from the Micheaux vault went to Omaha. As I understand it, again, I was not there, the cabinet came out of the armored car and was trundled into the vault there. The cabinet was opened and the drawers with the rubies and sapphires were removed. The tray with the diamonds was not removed because it was going on to Kansas City. The cabinet was relocked and put back into the armored car. The armored car was loaded with some other items and went to Kansas City. The cabinet did not get out of the armored car again until the armored car got to Kansas. Then it came out and was opened in the GemPrint operation there. That's when and where the diamonds were discovered to be missing."

"Did you check with the armored car company to see if there had been any other stops?"

Then Walrus cut in. "That's when I got involved."

Noonan looked at Walrus. "Take it away."

Walrus watched as Noonan scribbled in his notebook. "I got the call the morning the diamonds were discovered missing. It was from the Missouri State Troopers. The tray of diamonds had arrived in the GemPrint facility but there were no diamonds inside. The envelopes with the writing were in the box but no diamonds."

Noonan looked at Brody. "Have you seen the empty envelopes?"

"Yes. They are authentic. And my initials are on the envelopes."

"Step by step," Noonan said to Walrus. "How were the diamonds transported?"

Walrus kind of shrugged. "The precious stones, all of them, were moved by a contract armored car company, Micheaux Transport and

Delivery, and taken directly to Omaha. I worked with the Nebraska Highway Police. There had been a few stops between Micheaux and Omaha but they were in the range of 60 to 90 seconds. Stops signs, railroad crossings and the like. They did pinpoint the stops on GPS and there were all legitimate stops. Very short."

Noonan looked at his notebook page as he wrote. "When the cabinet with the gems got to Omaha, the cabinet was taken out of the back of the armored card. Correct?"

"Yes," Walrus assured him. "Under lock and key. The cabinet was not opened until it was in a secure room there. Their usual procedure. Then the precious stones were divided. Rather, the drawers were divided. All three drawers were taken out and put in a locked room. That's where the jewelry professionals would go over the gems. The drawer with the diamonds was slid back into the cabinet and the cabinet was locked. The diamonds in the drawer replaced in the cabinet were put back in the back of the armored car. The same one. For the night. The next day, the same three people, two women and a man, got into the armored and headed south. Nothing was taken out of the back of the armored car and the three did not take anything out of the armored car."

Noonan looked at Walrus, "You saw this on the security footage?"

"Every second. From the time the armored came into the holding facility until it left. And by that I mean, on the security footage I visually followed the cabinet out of the back of the armored car, into the holding area and then back into the armored car. Then I watched the opening of the cabinet, the removal of the three drawers, the replacement of the drawer with the diamonds, and the cabinet being locked again."

"So the diamonds were in the back of the same armored car that had come from the Micheaux vault."

"Yes," Walrus said. "Under lock and key and like I said, I have seen the security tapes. The cabinet with the diamonds was untouched during the entire time."

"Did anyone enter the armored car garage during the time the diamonds were there?"

"Yes, in and out. It's a secure area but only as far as people not employed by Micheaux Transport and Security. A lot of people. But they were all on tape. There was nothing out of the ordinary. I sat through about nine hours of surveillance footage. Nothing out of the ordinary."

Noonan looked at his notes. "How about the trip from the armored car depot to the GemPrint facility in Kansas City?"

"That," Walrus said wistfully, "is complicated. There were eight stops along the way. That is, the diamonds did not go directly to the GemPrint facility. There were stops along the way at banks and a jewelry store. Eight of them. But the cabinet with the diamonds did not leave the back of the armored car and there was no sign of tampering."

"But at least the same three drivers and crew had the diamonds in their possession." Noonan asked.

"Yes."

"How were the diamonds locked in the drawer?"

Brody cut in. "Let me answer that," he said to Walrus. As he spoke he produced a key which appeared like an oblong rectangle. "This, Heinz, is the key to the diamond drawer. The drawer with the diamonds, not the cabinet itself. It's a one-of-a-kind. That is, the code is one-of-a-kind. I locked the diamond drawer in the Micheaux vault with this key. The other key, the one that opened the diamond drawer, was sent to the GemPrint facility ahead of time. Once the drawer is locked, it can only be opened by one of two keys, the one I had and the one in Missouri."

"How about the two drawers for the other stones?"

"Same thing," Brody said. "But I did not have the key to those drawers, Attucks did. The other key, the second one, had been sent to the Omaha jewelry appraiser. The third copy went to the GemPrint Facility in Kansas City. There were only six keys and they were electronically set so the open/close code was not the same for each trip. Attucks had one in Micheaux. The jeweler in Omaha had three, one to open the cabinet and two for the two precious gem drawers. The GemPrint facility also had a key to the cabinet and a key to the diamond drawer. Six total."

Noonan scribbled a large question mark in his notebook. "If it is electronic, can it be hacked?"

Brody dangled the key. "Anything can be hacked. But you would have to be very clever to do it. On top of that, you would have to know the diamonds were being transferred. And which drawer to hack. None of us in the Micheaux vault knew the route the diamonds were going to take. I didn't and I do not believe Attucks did either. Yes, it is possible the drawer could have been hacked but there is no indication on the electronic record that the drawer had been opened or the armored car stopped anywhere long enough for the cabinet to be hacked and the gems stolen. But if there had been thieves, they would have taken the diamonds along with the rubies and sapphires."

"Were there security cameras in the armored cars?"

"No," replied Walrus. "But it is unlikely anyone associated with the transfer knew what was in the diamond drawer much less how to sell diamonds. Armored car crews are vetted pretty heavily and watched carefully."

Noonan kept writing and then asked what happened when the diamond drawer got to the GemPrint facility.

"I went over their procedure there," Walrus said. "Along with some Missouri State Trooper forensic people. We watched the security camera footage of the cabinet being unloaded and placed on a flatcar. It was pushed out of the garage and into the waiting area. A secure area, let me assure you. Then the cabinet was unlocked. Someone from a side room came with the electronic key for the diamond drawer. He did something with it, probably entering a code, and then pulled out the diamond drawer, the last one in the cabinet. It slid out and he opened the drawer. Then you could see the technicians opening envelope after envelope and then helplessly looking at the security cameras. Supervisors were called in. The drawer was relocked and stayed that way for about an hour. Then the Missouri State Troopers and some insurance agents arrived. The drawer was opened again and examined, top and bottom. It was eventually pulled apart to make sure the diamonds had not been slipped into a false bottom."

"And they found nothing?" Noonan asked flatly.

"That's right," Walrus said. "As they say where I grew up, zip. Nothing. Goose egg."

CHAPTER 5

To himself, Noonan mumbled, "Been there, done that."

After years in the field, he knew his best source of immediate information was going to be an insurance company. It did not really make any difference what anyone *thought;* what mattered was who was going to be paying the bill. There are three reasons investigators like to deal with insurance companies. First, they have no loyalty to anyone. Second, they can get documents which the police cannot. Third, they want the case wrapped up as soon as possible – as quietly as possible with no payout from the company.

Jeremy Saxton turned out to be the perfect insurance investigator. He was the kind of a man who came up through the ranks. He started as a salesman so he had the smoothness of a corporate executive with the cold-bloodedness of a pit viper. He was cool, calculating and a no-non-sense investigator. Even more important, he was black. And not just black as in the color of a paper bag. He was deepest, darkest Africa black.

"I hope you don't mind working with a black," was the first thing he said to Noonan.

"Don't care what color you are," Noonan replied with a smile. "As long as you live up to your reputation, I'm happy."

"What reputation is that?" Noonan's comment clearly set Saxton back a bit.

"Saxton, please," Noonan shook a finger at him comically. "This is a huge case. We are talking 63 diamonds which vanished in thin air. Loss to the insurance company could be in the millions. The insurance company is going to send its best. That's you. So, let's not talk race; let's talk criminals. What do you have?"

"What do you mean, 'What do I have?'"

Noonan was standing over a table in the basement of the bank where he had set up his command center. Walrus had departed to bring in the head of security for the armored car company in Sioux Falls that handled the transfer of the diamonds. Brody had gone to find a jeweler to verify the precious gems which had been delivered were, in fact, precious gems and not substitutes. Noonan was going over the official statements of the Missouri and Iowa police and patrol and troopers had taken from the armored car drivers and guards.

Noonan looked at Saxton with a been-there-done-that look. "Saxton, I'm not the enemy. I'm the one trying to save your company millions of dollars. There's no reason for us not to get along. You did not show up here just to say howdy. What I need is as much information as possible. What I have here," Noonan stretched his arm over the interviews, "are the interviews from the guards and bank staff. They are all DKNs, 'Don't Know Nothing.' I'm betting you have better paperwork." Noonan pointed to the folder under Saxton's arm.

Saxton smiled. "You know, I think we'll get along just fine."

Noonan smiled. "Good." Then he pointed at the folder under Saxton's arm. "The folder."

Saxton sat down in a chair beside the table and spread out the sheets of paper from the folder. "We did a background check on everyone who had anything to do with the missing diamonds. A lot of interesting tidbits but I'm afraid no solid leads."

"I like interesting tidbits."

Saxton leaned back in the chair and pointed at the papers on the table. "The only one getting rich is Ambrose Brody. Clean record, no criminal charges, owns a home here in Sioux Falls. And I mean owns as in he paid it off. Modest, nothing fancy. Wife is Jewish, which I found humorous more than interesting, has three children. His bank account and investments show he earned his money over the years, no sudden arrival of cash."

Noonan smiled. "That's good to know. If his wife is Jewish that must have raised some eyebrows with his family in Saudi Arabia."

"Probably the reason he's still in the United States," Saxton said. "Here nobody cares about you until it comes to money. When you have it, everyone loves you."

"Welcome to the real world," Noonan kind of squinted as he turned his head sideways. "Go on."

"Walrus is clean as a whistle, no bad boy youth. College graduate from Iowa State. Sixteen years on the force. Straight as an error. Wife and two kids, one of them, one of the kids, has problems. Drugs and DUIs. Is in a rehab house in California."

"How about me?" Noonan tapped his chest with his pen.

Saxton gave Noonan the innocent 'who me?' look.

"Don't give me that guff," Noonan said. "If you're good at your job, you did a background on me."

"W-e-l-l-l," Saxton began.

"Give," Noonan said.

Reluctantly Saxton *gave*. "Nothing bad, let's just say. Six years in the Army, one Article 15 for refusing to follow a directive."

"I was right. I still am."

"No big deal. Getting an Article 15 is sometimes a badge of honor. I've got six."

"You bad boy!"

"I know. But I can live with it."

"What else?"

"Married 52 years, two kids, no priors, owns a home in Sandersonville, have a reputation for solving unsolvable crimes .."

"I've been lucky."

"Lucky? With, what 146 cases solved? You are modest."

"Modest and still lucky. Keep going."

"No red flags. No priors, not pendings, no money."

"It's the 'no money' part that hurts the most."

"Tell me about it. In my next life I want rich parents."

"So do I. Now, a tough question. You're black. Kankan Musa was black. Is there a connection?"

Saxton laughed. "That crossed my mind when I got the call to get involved. The quick answer, no. I'm lead for the company and this is the biggest case in our history. Second, Kankan Musa may have been black and been proud of being black and his black heritage but that's as far as it went. He kind of/sort of adopted six children, all foster children, from Sioux Falls and all different races. They have moved on in life and now his family," Saxton made quote marks in the air with his fingers, "has grown to 31. There are also long-term employees or contractors, choose your own term, who may have been promised a slice of the Kankan Musa pie. None have anything in writing."

"Ah, a big happy family." Noonan chuckled.

"So, to answer your question, no. Me being back and Kankan Musa being black is just a coincidence."

Noonan waited for a moment, trying to figure out how to ask the next question. Saxton was as good as they get. "I know. The answer is three."

"Three?"

"You were wondering if I represent the only insurance company involved and if the other two are, shall we say, credible."

"You are good," Noonan said clearly impressed.

"Just like you," Saxton looked at him sideways. "I've been lucky. There are three insurance companies involved." He paused and then continued. "If the diamonds are not recovered. There is Micheaux bank insurance company which has washed its hands of this matter. The Micheaux Transport and Delivery has a crackerjack agent. I am the agent for the insurance company for all GemPrint outlets."

"I see," Noonan said. "Let me guess, you speak for all three insurance agencies?"

"Uh, no. The insurance company representing the Micheaux bank has said the gems left its vault so it is out of the matter. The insurance company representing Micheaux Transport and Delivery is one woman who is overworked and is letting me run with the ball. I am doing the heavy lifting."

Noonan smiled. "OK, my question has been answered. Even though I did not get a chance to ask it."

Saxton smiled. "I'm here to serve."

"Great." Noonan pointed to Saxton's paperwork. "Back to the basics. Anything interesting?"

"You law and order types are no-nonsense, I must say. Yes, three individuals. One bank Vice President, at this bank as a matter of fact, has a felony record for, get this, bank robbery."

"And he was hired here?!"

"His father owns the bank."

"That says a lot. How long ago was the robbery?"

"Twenty-five years ago."

"How much did he get?"

"Nothing. It was a stunt to show his father that the bank could be robbed. He was able to get about a million dollars transferred electronically to an account in another bank. Then he called the feds to report his own theft."

"I don't know if that's smart or stupid," Noonan smiled.

"The feds thought it was stupid and booked him."

"Let me guess, all charges dropped."

"Nope, served 200 hours of community service and was on probation for two years."

"A very bad boy, eh?"

"So far so good. No unexplained money in investments, married a Mormon and is a regular in church or, I guess, temple. Six kids so, if anyone needed money, he does. But he does not have any link to the diamonds, just the precious stones and none of them are missing."

"Well, you never know. We'll have to have a talk with him. What's his name?"

"Horatio Fagan. And he works for the Fitzsimons Bank and Trust."

"I thought you said his father ..."

"He married better."

Noonan shook his head. "The way of the world. You said there were three people to keep an eye on."

"Number Two is Attucks Musa. And he is a real piece of work. He's the lead for the probate distribution of the Kankan Musa estate."

"He was the one who opened the vault for the armored car guards to take the precious stones."

"Probably," Saxton pointed to a sheet of paper. "Let me say this diplomatically. Nicely, that is. Generally speaking, he is regarded as a sleazy, disreputable individual with the ethics of a rattlesnake and trustworthiness of a hungry alligator."

"Nice fellow. Who told you that?"

"Oh, everyone. He is universally disliked, distrusted and disdained. One person said it best, 'he'd chase a dime onto a crowded freeway.'"

"Nice guy. Who made the comment about the dime on the freeway?"

"Everyone. More or less."

"How'd he end up as the probate lead for the estate?"

"He's the oldest foster child and was made executor of the estate by Kankan Musa."

"Kankan Musa made him the executor?!"

"All the court can go on is paperwork. He was made executor 27 years ago. Probably before Kankan Musa realized what a piece of work Attucks was. If there was another paper naming another executor, it has not been found."

"It could have," Noonan wiggled his fingers of his right hand and allowed the hand to rise into the ether, "disappeared."

"Could have," Saxton said. "But as far as the court is concerned, Attucks is the executor and no one can prove otherwise. So he's in the catbird seat."

"Let me guess," Noonan said slyly. "The insurance company for the Micheaux Bank that is dodging responsibility is represented by Attucks."

"Bingo." Saxton shook his head. "The only saving grace for Attucks and his insurance company is the diamonds were provably in the envelopes before they were loaded into the armored car on its way to Kansas City. That kind of puts him and the Micheaux insurance company in the clear."

"No one is in the clear yet," Noonan said. "The banker is Number One suspect. Attucks is Number Two. Who's Number three?"

"This one's a beaut."

CHAPTER 6

"What took you so long?" Haysbert Nivon was the spitting image of Cary Grant. A very old Cary Grant but the two could have been peas in a pod. Considering his past, he and Cary Grant were peas in the pod for the movie TO CATCH A THIEF.

"And don't say I look like an aged Cary Grant. I do and we are not related. The only things we have in common are our age, I'm 82, the same age as Grant was when he died, and I was a real jewelry thief."

"That's not something someone admits to," Noonan said slyly. "In a town as small as Sioux Falls, it's a bet everyone knows."

"You got it," Nivon said as he figuratively shot Noonan with the two fingers of his right hand. "But you do have one thing wrong. Every jewelry theft west of the Mississippi gets dropped on my doorstep. I am either the expert the FBI calls or the suspected mastermind."

"You did have a sterling record as a jewelry thief," Noonan said.

"Please, Captain. Sterling is silver. My record was golden. I made a few mistakes and they tripped me up. I spent my time in prison, ghastly place, and I've been on the law and order payroll ever since."

"No kidding," said Noonan as he flipped pages in the report Saxton had provided. "Let's see, guilty of 18 thefts …"

"… the only ones they could prove," Nivon quickly added.

"A lot of the money was never found. What do you know about that?"

"I lived very well," Nivon said and the raised both hands to indicate the room where he was sitting behind a desk covered with files. "Too well. Spent every dime I had. Always figured I could get more. I could. Until one day I couldn't."

"So here you are, a private security consultant, in Sioux Falls."

"I was in the Witness Protection Program. But that was a while back. Too long ago. I've outlived all the nefarious individuals I flipped on. There was no money in the Witness Protection Program. I could not go back to my previous occupation so I opened this business. Now, as I tell all my clients, ..."

"That's not the way this works," Noonan started to say but Saxton cut him off.

"Actually, it is. We have put Mr. Navon on retainer."

"Call me Cary! Everyone else does!"

Noonan looked at both Saxton and Navon. "Mr. Navon ..."

"Cary!"

"OK, Cary. This is pretty serious stuff. We're talking millions."

"Captain, I am being serious. But it's funny, you know. I made millions and spent it as fast as I made it. The only thing that has changed are the faces of the people committing the felonies. I love them. They keep me from going broke. Odd, you know. I'm actually saving money by sitting on the other side of the table than these people. So, yes, I am serious. But it's funny. So, since you want to nuts-and-bolts, here you go."

Navon paused for a moment as he looked at Saxton. Saxton nodded and handed Navon some papers. Navon waved them aside. Then he looked at Noonan. "Captain, jewelry robberies are the same old same old. There are only so many ways to do it. The big problem is not figuring out how it was done, it is prosecuting the thieves. I made it easy because I was young and stupid. Even the most experienced thieves leave behind clues. Either at the crime scene or cashing out. And if they are ever caught, well, they're paying the IRS for centuries."

Navon pointed at the papers from Saxton he had shunted aside. "You want to solve the crime, got back to the basics. I don't even have to look at those papers to give you clues. Just an overview of the crime is enough for me. First, how do you know the diamonds actually existed at all in the first place? This could be a case of the owner of the gems and appraiser cutting a deal under the table. The gems supposedly disappear. The owner of the gems gets the insurance money and the appraiser gets the stones. The stones have not been GemPrinted so they can be sold anywhere."

Navon paused and then continued. "Even if the owner of the gems had not cut a deal under the table, how do you know the appraiser, actually saw the diamonds? Or whoever was handling the stones, actually put the stones in the little envelopes? Did anyone see him put the stones in the envelopes? Or do you just have his word he put the diamonds in the envelopes? And if he did put the diamonds in the envelopes, why are just the diamonds missing? That should be a clue."

Navon took a drink of the coffee from the mug he had on the table. He saw Noonan looking at the coffee and said, "I drink it all day. It doesn't affect me."

"I can't drink after about one in the afternoon," Noonan replied. "Otherwise I'm up all night."

Navon laughed. "I can drink coffee all day. But more than one glass of wine at night and I am toast!" He laughed. "Considering what I used to drink all night, I'm a lightweight."

"We all get old," Saxton cut in. "If I drank like I used to I'd be dead."

All three men laughed.

"Continuing," Navon said as the laugher died to a chuckles. "Are you sure the armored car guards actually loaded the correct cabinet into the armored car? They did not know which cabinet contained the diamonds. Maybe they were told to load an empty cabinet and the real cabinet with the diamonds was left behind. Or maybe the rubies and sapphires were put in one cabinet and the diamond drawer in another. Then the appraiser went back later and took the diamonds. Then there's the possibility the drawer was stripped of diamond in one of the armored cars. The idea that someone could not hack an electronic lock is a myth. I knew 12-year-olds who could open any electronic lock, sometimes faster than someone with the code. If one of the guards was left alone in the back of the armored car, he could have hacked the lock and dumped the diamonds into his pocket. It could be done in a few minutes. Maybe not all the diamonds at the same time, but in three or four minute intervals. When the other guard in the back was out getting deposits. As long as the thief does not get stupid like I did, he could get away with it."

"What about the armored car vaults where the drawers were held overnight?" Noonan asked.

"Poppycock," snapped Navon. "Captain, stop thinking like a cop. Or a criminal, for that matter. Whoever did this was one clever fellow. Whoever it was, knew it was necessary to get a squadron of possible suspects. There is safety in numbers because of the chaos."

Saxton looked at Noonan and then Navon. "If you were in my shoes, what would you do?"

Navon smiled. "The first thing to do is what all good cops do." He looked at Noonan and said, "You go back to the beginning and look around. I'd start with the heirloom bodies, the rings and bracelets and whatever. Make sure they existed. If there are still in existence, which I doubt, see if you can match up some of the precious stones with the bodies. At least that will tell you there really were diamonds to disappear."

"You said 'if they are still in existence,'" Noonan said to Navon. "Do you think the person who orchestrated the scam got rid of the bodies?"

"Absolutely! When you take gems out of heirlooms, it's for the money. The heirloom bodies with no gems are just dollars with no homes. I would expect them to be sent to the assay office right away. Particularly if there is a probate judge waiting for an indication of value. So, no, I don't think the person who ordered the bodies melted is automatically the mastermind but I do believe the melting of the bodies was a part of the scheme. Someone knew what they were doing. Everyone should be considered a suspect."

CHAPTER 7

Rachel Sandusky was exactly the kind of a suspect cops hate to interview. She was innocent of all charges, suggestions, insinuations or hypotheticals presented to her. She was the personification of innocence. In the law and order parlance of the day, she was a DKN, "Don't know nothing." She, allegedly, knew absolutely nothing about how her two ex-husbands, sequentially, had been able to maintain such a rich lifestyle on their incomes working for a string of armored car companies. It could not be proven that she was involved in any shenanigans or, as a matter of fact, any of those of her husbands.

Either of them.

Sequentially.

But the fact of the matter was that, *sub rosa,* law enforcement had been informed that any loss of valuables at any of the armed car companies was "not a problem" by six separate insurance companies. That being said, it did not take a Sherlock Holmes to peek behind the curtain. There were losses and the insurance companies picked up the tab. The losses were low enough that the alleged-but-never-prosecuted individuals were simply told to find employment elsewhere. They did and history repeated itself. The best John Law could do was pass the names of the alleged-but-never-prosecuted individuals on to the legal nemesis of all perpetrators: the IRS. One at a time, sequentially, the husbands found themselves in prison for income tax evasion. But there was not a word, above board or sub rosa, that the two husbands, sequentially, had ever been found to be culpable to any degree in any of the six separate incidences which insurance companies had stated "was not a problem."

Rachel Sandusky, who swore she knew absolutely nothing about her husbands' – both of them – peccadillos. Proof of that was she remained unindicted. She was on husband Number Three and he worked hard for an armored car company – and the one for which he currently worked – was the Micheaux Transport and Delivery out of Micheaux, South Dakota.

Rachel Sandusky reminded Noonan of the visual joke on the internet showing a knock-out young woman standing next to a convertible Maserati. The caption beneath the photograph read "The one on the left will cost you five times as much as the one on the right." The Maserati was on the right side of the photograph.

"I know why you are here," Sandusky said seductively as Noonan and Walrus sat down on her living room sofa. "We're a small state," she said as she looked at Noonan. "Nothing happens in this state that everyone does not know about. We are not really a state; we are a small town on a very long road."

She smiled.

Noonan smiled.

Walrus had the look of "been there done that."

"Well," Noonan said in the professional law and order tone, "then we don't have to do the usual preliminaries."

"OK," she said. "For the record, I know nothing about the disappearing of the diamonds and neither does my husband. He's at work now and I'm sure you'll talk to him at some point. He'll be back in town at about four this afternoon. Yes, he was one of the three employees of Micheaux Transport and Delivery that picked up the precious stones and no, he had no part in any nefarious scheme to steal diamonds. I and my husband have already spoken with the Walrus, she indicated Walrus with a tip of her head. "So I'll say the same thing now I said to him." Again the tip of her head. "We know nothing about the disappearing diamonds."

"Fine," Noonan said and then tried an obtuse approach. "Micheaux Transport and Delivery is out of Micheaux. That's a ways from here. There are probably more than a handful of armored car delivery services out of Sioux Falls. Why is your husband working for an armored car company out of Micheaux?"

Sandusky gave Noonan a tired look. "Captain, it is Captain, correct?"

"It will work."

"Captain, you are not from South Dakota. We are not like Kansas or other states that have lots of people. We have less than one million people – total. That's about one-sixth of the population of your state, North Carolina. We're one-third the population of Kansas and are about the same size. In square miles, that is. So, when it comes to businesses that are not selling a product, the services need to move about the state. We have two, what you in the East, call metropolitan areas: Rapid City and Sioux Falls. They are 350 miles between the two and a lot of nothing in between. Micheaux Transport and Delivery offers armored car service in and around Sioux Falls." She paused and then continued. "I'm also betting you see some kind of a link between the city of Micheaux where the diamonds were and Kansas City where the diamonds were discovered missing and the fact that the armored car services is named Micheaux."

"As a matter of fact," Noonan said. "Yes."

"What do you know about Micheaux, the city?"

"Just what you tell me."

Sandusky was the perfect woman-splaner. There was not a hint of tiredness or looking down on the questioner. It was if she was giving a child a history lesson. "Before the 1950s the city was named Combine. Then it went broke. About a decade later it was bought by a black who had changed his name to reflect his heritage, Kankan Musa. He had made a lot of money in a lot of land and industrial ventures. He then proceeded to bring the city back to life. He understood economics as well as any professor of economics. Better, I'd guess you say, because he actually made the economy better rather than talking about it. Rather than buying what the city needed from Sioux Falls he set up small businesses in his city, now Micheaux. Then he went one step better. He had the city print its own money. Just like the mining days of old. Everything and anything you wanted to buy in Micheaux was bought and sold with Micheaux script, called Micheauxs."

Noonan shook his head. "I'd have said that was counterfeiting."

"Not according to the United States government. A state cannot print its own money. That's in the United States Constitution. But cities can. It's one of those 'it's not illegal' items. As long as the Micheauxs were not used to avoid taxes and could be converted to United States dollars, the script is legal. If you live in Micheaux, you get paid in Micheauxs and pay your bills in Micheaux. If you live outside of the city, you are paid in United States dollars by direct deposit."

"So there's no American cash in Micheaux?" Noonan asked.

"Oh, there's cash there, yes. Smaller amounts for coffee, candy bars and there are some fast food outlets. But there's no bank like there are in most small towns. The old bank that went belly-up in Combine was brought back to life but it is more of a bookkeeping operation. When you are paid, your Micheauxs are put on your balance sheet at the bank. When you make a purchase, it comes off the balance sheet. It's all electronic so there is no needed dig around in your wallet at the grocery store."

"Then," Noonan said as he examined his notebook, "why does Micheaux need an armored car service."

"Because it is more than just an armored car service. It only has three armored cars. The rest of the fleet is transport trucks. To specifically answer your question, there is still a lot of valuable property that requires moving. Jewelry, for instance. Then there are furs, heirlooms and investment gold. Those deliveries are not every day but the cost of delivery from Sioux Falls was prohibitive. It made no sense to call an armored car company in Sioux Falls to come to Micheaux to pick up an item and take it to Sioux Falls. When that happened, you would have to pay for the armored car service in Sioux Falls for two trips, one when it was running empty. So Kankan Musa set up his own delivery service. It's based in Micheaux but it makes deliveries all around Sioux Falls. Only a few of those are in the armored cars. The rest are trucks. They move furniture, groceries, liquor, office supplies, homewares."

"But you live here," Noonan leaned his head to the side to indicate the room in which they were sitting.

"Correct. The bulk of the business of the armed car company is around Sioux Falls so there is a service center here. Trips to Micheaux are only as needed, usually on Tuesdays or Thursdays. Between delivery dates, items are warehoused here in Sioux Falls."

"So," Noonan said as he scribbled, "on any day your husband could be anywhere around Sioux Falls. How is it he was on the trip to Micheaux when the diamonds disappeared."

"I didn't say he was. But, anticipating your question, he was. Just the luck of the draw. There are 12 employees, half of them in the armored car end of the busines. He got the call on Wednesday to be in Micheaux on Thursday morning early for a pickup. He was not told what the pickup was."

"So he had no idea he was picking up diamonds?"

"I took the call. So, no, he didn't know and I didn't know."

"And you have no idea how the diamonds could have vanished?"

"Not a clue."

Noonan looked at Walrus with the it's-time-to-go look. As he stood up, he asked one more question. "Have you ever been to Micheaux?"

"I used to live there. I transferred with my husband here to Sioux Falls when the armored car business picked up."

"When was that?"

"Three years ago."

"I notice you are wearing some fine jewelry."

"Thank you."

"Did you have that jewelry when you lived in Micheaux?"

"Some of them, yes, Why?"

"I was just wondering," Noonan said as he put his notebook away. "Banks do more than just transfer money. They have vaults for jewelry," he pointed to her necklace, "and safety deposit boxes. The missing diamonds started in a vault. Is the vault in Micheaux in the bank?"

"Yes, but it's an odd answer. When the city of Combine was Combine, the bank was very small because the city was very small. Micheaux is now, oh, ten times the size of Combine. So the bank expanded into what was then cold storage refrigeration for the old slaughterhouse. The walls were reinforced and vault doors were installed. It's not as secure as a vault in Omaha or Kansas City, for instance, but it still has all the surveillance equipment of a big city bank."

"Has it ever been robbed?"

"No. And the diamonds from the bank vault did not disappear in the vault. They were checked before they left the vault. Didn't your Muslim appraiser tell you that?"

CHAPTER 8

While Rachel Sandusky was cucumber cool, her husband, Daniel Sandusky, was Trinidad Scorpion *Moruga* chili pepper hot. He had no fuse at all. When he was ushered into the conference room of Micheaux Transport and Delivery, he took one look at Walrus and exploded.

It was expletives tumbling over each other like an act in *Cirque du Soleil* for a good thirty seconds. That's when he took a breath.

Then he started again.

Noonan waited until Daniel Sandusky needed another breath and then indicated Walrus ought to vacate the room. Then Sandusky lit into Noonan. Noonan waited until Sandusky stopped for a third breath and then pointed to an empty chair beside one of the table.

"Do you know what a skeleton fears more than any other thing on the planet?"

Sandusky stalled and did a doubletake. Noonan pointed to the empty chair again. Then he leaned forward and said, "a dog." Sandusky thought a split second and then smiled.

"Got me there. Now, who the …"

"Noonan," Noonan said as he held out his hand for a shake. "And I'm here to get you off the hook."

"Ain't possible," snapped Sandusky, his anger slow ebbing away.

Noonan sat down. "When a crime is committed, anything is possible. But, as I am sure you know now, until the crime is solved, well, everyone's a suspect."

"No shin Sherlock."

"Shin?"

For the first time since Noonan entered the room, Sandusky smiled. "Gotta watch the language on the job."

Noonan smiled. "Shin will do it. Now, Daniel, can I call you Daniel?"

"Dan is better."

Noonan indicated the empty chair again and this time Sandusky sat down. Noonan settled in an empty chair across the table from him and pulled a notebook out of his briefcase.

"Dan, I'm not going to give you the law and order song and dance. I just want as much information from you as possible. Then I'm going to go away and see if I can solve this crime. If I can, you'll never see me again."

"Have I heard that before," snapped Sandusky.

Noonan shook his head sadly. "Dan, cops do not believe anyone. That's why you always tell the truth as soon as possible. Then they go away and do not come back.

"I spent three hours with, with, with..." and he pointed through the wall at an invisible Walrus.

"I can't change the past, Dan. All I can do is work to solve the crime so we can all get on with our lives. So, give me a rundown of your involvement and I'll see if I can make this as painless as possible."

"You've already failed."

"Well," Noonan smiled. "I'll keep trying to make it as painless as possible. Tell me what I want to know and I'll be gone. Let's start with why you made the initial pickup in Micheaux. Why didn't another armored car company make the pickup? You basically picked up the gems and diamonds from the Micheaux Bank and delivered them to another city."

Sandusky seemed to relax. "I'll tell you the same thing I told whateverhisname is," he said pointing through the wall again. "The City of Micheaux strongly supports local hire. Micheaux Transport and Delivery is local."

"But you live in Sioux Falls."

"I do now. But Micheaux Transport and Delivery is headquartered in Micheaux. It has a number of vehicles which make pickups and delivery all over the area."

"Are all the trucks housed in Micheaux?"

"If you mean does every pickup and delivery start in Micheaux, no. The company is headquartered there; the armored can be anywhere."

"Where is anywhere?"

"As I am sure you know, …"

"Actually, I don't know anything. Why don't you educate me?"

"That's a first. A cop who doesn't know anything."

Noonan laughed.

Then Sandusky laughed.

"OK, Cop. Here you go. Micheaux Transport and Delivery started out as a local operation. Micheaux needed a lot of things brought in so rather than hire an outside trucking firm, that is, a transport company from outside the city, it started its own company."

"The city?"

"Kankan Musa. He was the city. He knew whether he paid for groceries to be brought in from Sioux Falls or sent a truck from Micheaux to get the groceries, the transportation cost was the same. But where the money was spent was not. Contracting with a transport company in Sioux Falls meant money leaving Micheaux. But with a transport company headquartered in Micheaux, all of the money spent on transportation stayed in town. The drivers spent their wages in Micheaux, the garage support people were paid locally and spent locally. I'm sure you know what I'm talking about."

Noonan smiled. "That's not what I asked. When the Micheaux armored cars are not in Micheaux, where are they located? I mean, the company does a lot of transport work around Sioux Falls."

"The company has three armored cars and six truck and trailer rigs. That many vehicles were too large for Micheaux so the company opened a Sioux Falls office. This one. When the vehicles are not being used, they are housed here. Anticipating your next question, no, we do not keep the cargo from the armored cars here. When we have that kind of cargo. Depending on where it is going, there are six secure depots in Sioux Falls we can use. The only cargo kept here is in trucks and trailers when delivery is the next day. Or delayed."

Noonan made a show of looking in his notebook. "Your wife says the two of you were living in Micheaux until about three years ago."

Sandusky shook his head. "I knew you'd bring her up. Her two ex-husbands were sleazy. Yeah, we got married seven years ago. She moved to Micheaux to get away from her two ex's crimes and their reputations. She used to live in Rapid City and moved to Micheaux because she did not want to leave South Dakota. She has investments in real estate she has to keep track of. That's where her money came from, by the way. Not me or either of her ex-husbands. She was living below the radar in Micheaux when I met her. I left the Army ten years ago and moved to Micheaux doing construction. When the trucking and transport business took off, they needed more people so I signed on."

Noonan was writing in his notebook. Looking at the page in his notebook he asked, "What kind of construction?"

"Not that it makes any difference, cement and plumbing primarily."

"No wiring or high-tech work?"

"Wiring, but nothing that involved computers. And, again, anticipating your question, nothing that had anything to do with security. Or the bank. That building was already up when I got to Micheaux. All of the work on the vault had been done before I got to Micheaux. That includes the surveillance equipment."

"Who put in the vault and surveillance equipment?"

"Don't know. Like I said, it was done before I got to Micheaux."

"Do you know who handled the surveillance equipment?"

"Sure. Attucks Musa. He handles all of the security around town."

"Musa? A relation to Kankan Musa?"

"Nephew. Changed his name to please his uncle. Happened long before I got to Micheaux."

Noonan fiddled with his pen. Sandusky cut into the silence. "Look, Cop, I know where you are coming from but I can tell you, whatever happened to those diamonds did not happen in Micheaux. At least not with regard to us, the armored car operators. Three of us. It's all on the surveillance camera. We arrived and stood outside the vault until we were invited in. Attucks and the diamond man pointed at a small cabinet and we loaded the cabinet into the truck. We drove the truck all the way to the Micheaux facility in Omaha. We did not stop along the way. There were two of us in the back. At our Omaha facility we unloaded the cabinet. It's on the security camera. That's it. EOS, end of story."

Noonan was writing furiously. Then he said, "So you only went into the vault after you had been invited inside, correct?"

"It's on the surveillance footage."

"How many people were inside the vault at that time?"

"Two. Attucks and the other guy, the appraiser."

"And the cabinet was locked when you go there."

"I don't know if it was locked. It was shut. It was not open when we were in the vault and it was not opened in the back of the armored. We delivered it, unopened, to our facility . If it was unlocked, I don't know. But we did not open it at any time it was in our possession."

CHAPTER 9

"You got more out of him that I did," Walrus said as the two sat in his unmarked and drove across Sioux Falls.

"It's my charm," Noonan said with sly smile and then added, "And I don't have a mustache."

"Mustaches never worked wonders, I'll have you know. But it sure adds to my evil look when I'm interrogating a perp."

"Size and body weight have a bit to add," Noonan said with a smile. "I've been told that being old helps. Kind of grandfatherly. I, of course, wouldn't know because I'm only 37."

"That's how old I'll be next year!"

They both laughed.

"Let me guess," Walrus said as he glanced at the ceiling of the unmarked. "It's to the Micheaux transport station in Omaha."

"You read me like a book, Walrus!"

"Not really. I've been in this business too long."

"We both have been. Nice thing, so to speak, is that things do not change. There is always a bad guy lurking in the shadows," Noonan said tiredly. "Fortunately, for me that is, there is same old same old. This is another one of my impossible crimes, something that could not have occurred but did."

"And someone made off with a whale of a lot of money."

"Odd for to use the word whale."

Both men laughed.

The ride to Omaha was pleasant but a wasted trip. Both men knew it but, when you are required to turn over every rock, you turn over every rock.

In one of his previous investigations, Noonan had worked with a Navy man. The two had been paired to create confusion, not cooperation. It had not worked. The two worked well in tandem and stopped the theft of 800 pounds of gold. During their brief time together, Noonan had picked up a few Navy terms which had served him well over the years. 'O' dark hundred,' for instance, was any time early in the morning. If someone asked when you got out of bed, you'd say it was 0' dark hundred rather than 02 hundred or 2 a.m. Another was the "Acey Deucey Club." This was when an officer assigns an enlisted man to do a chore while the officer goes for a beer. But his favorite Navy term was "to sandpaper the anchor." This means doing a meaningless task which had no redeeming value.

In Omaha, Noonan and Walrus sanded the anchor. After watching footage of the armored arriving, they watched for an hour as the armored sat in the secured area waiting for another load. There was some kind of a problem with paperwork as three women – two drivers and a security guard – argued about something. An item came out, about the size of a briefcase. Then the cabinet came out.

Walrus and Noonan interviewed the woman who had argued with the drivers. Nannette Stevenson was reserved and overly cautious when she spoke with them. Even after Micheaux Transport and Delivery confirmed both Walrus and Noonan were law enforcement, she was cautious.

"I'm not in the trusting business," Stevenson said flatly to Noonan. "Maybe I can answer your questions, maybe I can't. You aren't local law enforcement."

"True," Noonan said casually. "But we don't want to know anything about your security measures. Just a few questions about your drivers and a delivery that was made about a week ago."

"Yeah," she said flatly. "The missing diamonds. I've been over and out and under and through with the FBI and the troopers and some insurance people. Why don't you look at what I said to them. It's the same thing I'm going to say to you."

"P-r-o-b-a-b-l-y," Noonan said stretching out his words. "Maybe we're going to ask questions you haven't answered."

"Maybe. Make it quick. I've got work to do."

Walrus tried to say something official but Noonan cut him off. "Ms Stevenson, keeping this as short as possible, do you know the drivers of the armored car who drove the diamonds here from Sioux Falls."

She gave him a disdainful look. "You're not from around here. Around here we know everyone and everyone's business. Micheaux Transport and Delivery is not that large. We all know each other. Yes, I know the drivers of the armored car that delivered the diamonds. They were the same ones who left here for Kansas City."

Noonan made a show of writing in his noted book.

Stevenson was having none of it.

"Don't fiddle in your notebook to impress me. My answers will be the same. Your questions are going to be the same. Yes, I knew the drivers. No, they did not stop anywhere along the way. No, no one in the armored car or, for that matter, working for Micheaux Transport and Delivery had a key to the cabinet containing the diamonds. Yes, the diamonds in the cabinet came through here. The cabinet was unloaded here and taken to a secure room. Two of the drawers were removed. The drawer with the diamonds was removed with the other stones but put back in the cabinet and the cabinet was placed back in the armored car. It was out of the armored car for about two hours but it was never out of a secure location. It's all on the security footage."

Noonan smiled but he kept on writing. "How do you know for certain the armored car from Sioux Falls did not stop along the way, even for lunch?"

"GPS. Look, there are three services we offer. One is intra-city. Bank to business to bank to business. We pick up and deliver valuables. On those trips the GPS just tells us there were a lot of stop-and-gos. Unless there is something to report, the journey is just paperwork.

Second, on longer trips, like the one from Micheaux, the armoreds are tracked on GPS. Now there are stops along the way – stoplights, railroad crossings, accidents, floods, construction zones – but those are called in so no one thinks there's a robbery in progress. The list of stops from Micheaux was turned over to the FBI. Don't you people talk among each other?"

This time Walrus cut in. "Usually, but just in case something was missing."

"Missing!" Stevenson was on the edge of anger. "The diamonds did not disappear while they were in our possession here in Omaha. The security footage proves it. The cabinet came in from Micheaux City. It arrived here and was opened to remove the three drawers. Two drawers were transferred to the jewelry appraiser here, the srawers with the precious stones. We know that because the jeweler who accepted the gems was here and signed the paperwork. The drawer with the diamonds was replaced in the cabinet. The cabinet was closed. The cabinet was relocked. The cabinet went back into the armored car and then on to Kansas City. It was not opened in the armored car along the way. No one had to key to open it and no armored was off the GPS grid long enough for anything to have happened. For us, it was another pass-through."

Noonan felt the need to ask one more question. "You said, 'pass-through.' What did you mean by that?"

Stevenson looked at him as if he were a stubborn child. "Officer, I'm assuming you do not know anything about the armored car business. Yes, we do carry cash. But that's only when the armoreds are in the cities. Contrary to your television programs, there's not that much cash out there. Everyone is using credit cards, debit cards, checks and order forms. Say, ten years ago there was a lot of cash in the armored cars. Not so today. We still service banks, credit unions, stores and malls. But that's local. Generally we move valuables from city to city that cannot be trusted to the United States Postal Service or the other delivery companies which I will not name. Those valuables include what you would call paperwork, computer hard drives, antiques and because we are climate controlled, valuables like furs, high priced liquor and occasionally body parts."

"Body parts?" Noonan was surprised.

"We don't publicize it but, yes, like hearts, kidneys, you know body parts. We can be door-to-door and, like I said, because we have temperature-controlled vehicles, we are the go-to service for surgeons. We don't advertise our services but they are available."

"I've never heard you did that," Noonan said.

"We don't advertise that we do," Stevenson snapped. "In a nutshell, to you and," she glanced toward Walrus, "local cops, the FBI and the insurance company investigating the vanishing of the diamonds," she made a whirling of her right index finger in the air. "The armored car from Micheaux did not stop on the way here for any one stop longer than maybe a minute. The same drivers who started the trip arrived here and left here for Kansas City. The cabinet with the gems was opened here, two drawers of gems were given to the jewelry connection here, the drawer with the diamonds was replaced, unopened, back in the cabinet. The cabinet was locked and replaced in the armored car. The armored car left for Kansas City. EOS, End of story. You want to see the security footage?"

CHAPTER 10

Noonan and Walrus spent the night in Omaha. The next morning, they headed south to Kansas City.

"Let me guess," Walrus said when he picked Noonan up, "You solved the case."

"Absolutely! Now we can both go back to chasing bad boys and girls."

Both men laughed.

The trip to Kansas City, Missouri was uneventful. Noonan commented he found it interesting, both historically and linguistically, that cities like St. Louis and Kansas City are in two states and divided by rivers. In the case of Kansas City – both of them – the rivers were the Kansas and Missouri while St. Louis – both cities – were dived by the Mississippi and Missouri rivers.

"I kind of live on the Missouri River," Walrus said in jest.

"Really?" Noonan asked.

"Yup," Walrus said. "Sioux Falls is on the Big Sioux River and it feeds into the Missouri River," he paused, "about 400 miles downstream."

Both men laughed.

"You know," Noonan said. "We could have taken a plane for this trip."

"And miss the wonders of Midwest?" Walrus said in jest. "Perish the thought."

Noonan laughed. "A lot of Indian names in this part of the country."

"Well," said Walrus. "There were a lot of Indians in this part of the country. Omaha is the name for the tribe that was there. Translates as 'Dwellers of the bluff.'"

"Let me guess, 'Sioux' translates as 'Sioux' for the Indians."

"Actually, no. There were seven Sioux nations at one time. Generally they are called Lakota or Dakota. That's what they call themselves. That's where the names for North and South Dakota came from. The word *Sioux* is actually a French corruption of a word from a local Indian dialect. As the story goes, a French explorer asked an Indian who was *not* a Sioux what was the name of those Indians up the river? The Indian, no friend of the Indians up the river that's for sure, said, in his language, they were "little snakes." The corruption of his term into French became the name *Sioux*. The term stuck."

"I'm sure the Lakota were not happy with that name."

"Still aren't," Walrus said.

CHAPTER 11

In Kansas City, the Micheaux Transport and Delivery parking facility was packed with personnel. What surprised Noonan were the three FBI agent. Noonan's experience with the FBI had been minimal. In Noonan's world, the FBI only appeared in the form of reports. When the FBI had something definitive, that *definitive* arrived as a report. But here in Kansas City there were three agents.

That being said, as Walrus told Noonan confidentially, "They will only be here as long as it takes to say their say and they will, poof, be gone in a puff of smoke."

Walrus was correct.

One FBI agent, who did not provide Noonan or Walrus with a business card, handed Walrus a form. As Walrus was looking at it, another agent said to Noonan, in a flat tone, "We have identified seven sets of fingerprints on the outside of the cabinet, five sets on the inside. The seven sets on the outside of the cabinet match the employees of the armored car company employees. The five sets of fingerprints on the inside of the cabinet were on the drawers to the cabinet. Two of them match the assayer who was in Micheaux. Ambrose Brody, and the security person in Micheaux, Attucks Musa. Neither of them have criminal records, federal or state. The other three sets were from the support staff at Kansas GemPrint. The missing diamonds were discovered in the GemPrint secure area. Only the diamonds were missing."

Noonan listened carefully and then asked, "Were there any fingerprints on the envelopes of the missing diamonds?"

"Yes," said another agent flatly. "Five sets."

"Were there any prints on the envelopes of the other precious stones?"

"Yes," again the flat response. "All envelopes were examined for fingerprints. The envelopes in Omaha were of Ambrose Brody, Attucks Musa and the employees of Omaha Gem Appraisals."

"And no other fingerprints were found on the inside of the cabinet? On any drawer or envelope."

"Correct. Just what I told you." Then the agent did what FBI agent always do. They repeat all of the facts.

Then, like the losses on a craps table, the three FBI agents were gone.

"Without so much as a howdy-do," Walrus said to Noonan as the agent left *en masse*. "Don't let the door hit your butt on the way out," he said to no one in particular.

"FBI's the same from sea to shining sea," Noonan said absently.

Now it was time to look at the security footage. Noonan and Walrus watched as the Micheaux Transport and Delivery armored car came into the Kansas City facility. The two women Walrus and Noonan had seen on the footage in Omaha stood beside the armored car while three other people, two men and a woman, signed paperwork. Then the armored car left the lot.

"Now the cabinet is on its way to Kansas City GemPrint," the station manager told Noonan and Walrus. "There were a handful of stops on the way, all of them about a minute long."

"Is there footage of the cabinet being unloaded at Kansas City GemPrint?" Noonan asked.

"Right here," and the manager put a disc into a computer on a table in the secure area of the warehouse.

Noonan and Walrus watched as the cabinet was unloaded in the garage of a facility with a huge sign that read KANSAS CITY GEMPRINT. The back door of the armored car was opened and the same drivers who had picked up the cabinet in Micheaux pulled out the cabinet. They turned it over to three people who were in the garage. Then the armored car left the back of the GemPrint facility. The cabinet was put on a flatbed cart and rolled through a set of double doors. It only stopped long enough for one of the three people to punch in a code to open the door. When the door opened, the three people and the cabinet went inside.

Noonan and Walrus watched the footage of the cabinet sitting by itself in the main room of Kansas City GemPrint for an hour before someone from Kansas City GemPrint came over to open it. She was not one of the three employees Noonan and Walrus had seen earlier. She clearly had a key because she used it to open the cabinet. Once the cabinet was opened, three employees pulled out the drawers. The three drawers were put on a nearby table. Noonan and Walrus watched as the drawers were opened.

For the next minute, nothing happened. Then an employee picked up one of the envelopes and opened it. There was a look of surprise on her face. She clearly found it empty. Clearly thinking it might be an error, she replaced the envelope and picked up the next one. It was empty too. The shocked look on her face was so pronounced Noonan and Walrus could see it on the grainy footage. Then pandemonium reigned. In the next minute every one of the envelopes which should have held diamonds were examined. They were all empty. The supervisor who had been standing with her arms crossed sprinted for a back wall where she pushed some kind of a button. Within a heartbeat, the back room was full of people, several of them with drawn weapons. Then the footage went black.

"Everything else is just people standing around with a surprised look on their face," the representative of Kansas City GemPrint told Noonan and Walrus. "Do you want to see any of the footage again?"

Noonan said yes and asked to see the transfer of the cabinet out of the armored car at the Kansas City GemPrint facility again. He watched it and then asked an odd question. "I notice the guards who unloaded the cabinet are wearing light jackets. I mean, I can see the roscoe bulges on these guards. As I remember, the guards in Omaha were wearing heavier jackets. They had their firearms on the outside, in holsters around their waist."

Walrus backed the footage up. "You're right. I'm surprised they even had light jackets. It's not cool this time of year. Probably to keep their firearms covered."

"Maybe," said Noonan thoughtfully. "Maybe."

CHAPTER 12

Nanette Stevenson was both annoyed and surprised to see Noonan and Walrus again. "Hey, I told you everything I knew. Why are you back here in Omaha?"

Noonan smiled like an absent-minded grandparent. "Sometimes I miss things that are obvious. We had to drive through Omaha so I thought we should stop. You were so helpful the last time we were here. Just a question I didn't ask before."

"Yeah?" It was not a pleasant tone.

Noonan continued his charade as the absent-minded grandfather. "When I watched the surveillance footage, the drivers coming in from Sioux Falls appeared to have on thick jackets. But on the footage in Kansas City, they were wearing light jackets. Did I miss something?"

"No," snapped Stevenson. "But what they wore has nothing to do with the missing diamonds."

"Probably," Noonan said. "But it's just one of those little things that cause problems. I just want to finish this investigation as soon as possible, you know. Let you get back to your regular job."

Stevenson gave him the look of a frustrated child. "OK, yes, they were wearing heavier jackets when they arrived here. One of the deliveries, it got off here in Omaha, was an organ donation. So the armored car had been refrigerated. After the organ was dropped off here, the back of the armored car did not have to be refrigerated. So the guards could remove their thick jackets and put on thinner ones."

"Did that have anything to do with the argument I saw on the surveillance footage?" Noonan asked.

"Just a complaint about the coldness of the armored car. One of the women in the back wanted to know why the cab was refrigerated if the organ was in a refrigerated container."

"Good question. Why?"

Stevenson got snippy. "Why?"

"Just interested. Seems logical to me."

"Well, I do not know. It's what we do with organ deliveries. I don't know if it's federal or state regulations but that's how we do it."

"Did the organ come from Micheaux City?"

"I don't know and I don't care."

"Fair enough. Just one more question. How often does Micheaux Transport and Delivery transfer organs?"

"I don't know and if I did, I would not tell you. It has nothing to do with the disappearing diamonds."

"Maybe not," Noonan said. "Maybe not."

Halfway back to Sioux Falls, Noonan got his answer.

Actually, Walrus did.

"The answer is yes," Walrus told Noonan after he hung up his cellphone. "The organ was a kidney. Where it was removed I do not know. But it was transferred to Micheaux and was scheduled to be moved in the same delivery with the diamonds."

"That," said Noonan flatly, "is v-e-r-y interesting."

CHAPTER 13

Whenever Noonan had a case, he had two, tried-and-true sources of information: history and the local newspapers. He began by looking up the history of Combine, the city that became Micheaux. There were a few references to it, but in the generic. There was nothing particularly important about it. When he punched the name of the city up on the internet he got references to the combine, a "factory on wheels" which served three separate functions at the same time: cutting wheat stalks, separating out the wheat berries, and then dumping the stalks – now called hay – back into the field so they could be collected and turned into bales. Combine, the city, vanished completely after the Second World War as agribusiness squeezed family farms out of existence all across the Midwest.

There were no references to Combine in any South Dakota newspaper Noonan parsed. Micheaux, the city, was not mentioned at all. Neither was Kankan Musa. Finding data on Micheaux, the man, the namesake was as easy as hitting "enter" on the key board. And it was impressive, clearly the reason for Kankan Musa to name the city after this significant South Dakota personality.

Oscar Devereaux Micheaux had been a giant in the film industry. But not the 'white' movie industry; the one which catered to black audiences. He established the first movie company owned by a black, the

Lincoln Motion Picture Company, and, as an independent producer, he brought 44 films to the big screen. He produced both silent and sound films and was generally viewed as the most successful black film producer in the Jim Crow era.

Micheaux had born on January 2, 1884 in Metropolis, Illinois. Noonan did not believe a community named Metropolis existed. It sounded more like the name of a city where Batman or Superman might live. In fact, he was in error. But it was a very small community. Today. And was probably much smaller in 1884. It was situated along the Ohio River in Massac County and, in 2010, had a population of 6,537. It had been settled by a French expeditionary force in 1757. A fort was built, *Fort de L'Ascension*, which fought off the Cherokees during the French and Indian War. Noonan found this tidbit odd because the French were allied with the Indians during that war, proof being the name of the war. The fort was destroyed but after the Revolutionary War, President Washington ordered it rebuilt. It was renamed Fort Massac. Its reputation was somewhat sullied in 1805 when General James Wilkinson and Vice President Aaron Burr met at the fort and planned what was later called Burr's attempt to form a new nation with himself as the leader. The city's position on the Ohio River made it a prime location for steamboat travel and long after Oscar Micheaux had died, it became the site of a Harrah's casino and hotel. It was currently the home of the Honeywell Uranium Hexafluoride Processing Facility, which converted uranium into hexafluoride for nuclear reactors.

Oscar Michaux, then without the 'e' in his last name, was the fifth of 13 children born on a farm to a former slave from Kentucky. His parents, strong advocates of education, moved into the city so their children could get an education. The family was able to make a go of it for a few years, but then they had to return to their roots. This did not go well with Oscar and he became rebellious. So rebellious, in fact, his father sent him into the city to do the marketing for the family's farmed product. Oscar liked the job of smooth talking clients and picked up the interpersonal skills he would need to be successful in the film industry.

At 17 he left Metropolis for the big city, in this case Chicago. He lived with an older brother who was a waiter. They did not get along because Oscar wanted more from life than a mundane job where nothing changed. He saved his money and moved out. He worked a variety of jobs including those in a stockyard and steel mill. After being "swindled out of two dollars" by an employment agency, he decided to go out on his own. That $2 would have been about $70 in current dollars. It may not have been much in present day dollar but it was a large enough amount to get Micheaux to become an independent entrepreneur. His started a shoeshine operation and then became a Pullman porter. The job as a porter was particularly important for three reasons. First, he traveled the United States so he had an understanding of the national business environment. Second, he learned to productively interact with all classes of people, black and white. Third, he could save money because he did not have to support a wife and children.

The third reason turned out to be a curse. He took his savings from working as a porter and worked as a homesteader in South Dakota. He was a successful as a farmer but only until he got married for the first time. His wife was unhappy with their lot which created tension at home. While he was away on business, she gave birth to their first child, drained their joint bank account and fled the farm. Then her father sold Micheaux's land and kept the money for himself.

Putting his personal disasters behind him, Micheaux decided it was time to change the direction of his life. The course he chose was writing and film making. He proceeded to write but it would not be until 1913 that his first book, THE CONQUEST: THE STORY OF A NEGRO PIONEER, made print. It was the story of a black homesteader and the economic and racial hardships a black homesteader faced. His second book to reach print, THE HOMESTEADER, caught the attention of the manager of the Lincoln Motion Picture Company in Los Angeles. The deal to make a movie of the book fell apart because Micheaux wanted artistic control. Rather than give up, Micheaux founded the Micheaux Film & Book Company of Sioux Falls. He started his film career with THE HOMESTEADER. To fund the film – and more than 40 others – he dug into his past to find the necessary production dollars. Those funds came from people he had met and befriended in his years as a Pullman porter. Surprisingly in the Jim Crow environment of the period, his pictures did well even though they focused on the difficulties of being black in an era of discrimination, mob violence and lynching. He died in 1951.

Noonan found the life of Micheaux impressive. Apparently James Clarkson, *aka* Kankan Musa, did as well. As it turned out, Kankan Musa was a good choice for the name change for Clarkson. Both were staggeringly rich. Kankan Musa, the original one, was the Emperor of Mali between 1312 to 1337, and in the days before Elon Musk, was the richest man in history. In current dollars, he was worth about $300 billion. A Muslim, in 1324 he made a pilgrimage to Mecca with 60,000 men. The procession included 12,000 servants each of whom carried about four pounds of gold. The train also included 80 camels, each carrying between 50 and 300 pounds of gold. Musa was quite generous along the way and spent so much gold that the metal was devalued for the next decade.

All of this history was interesting but did not offer Noonan a clue as to the disappearing of the diamonds. The community of Micheaux did not have a newspaper and Noonan could not find any article on Micheaux, Clarkson or Musa in South Dakota papers. An internet search gave him nothing but the historical background of the city of Micheaux and Clarkson's name change.

The only link Noonan could see that might be productive between the history of the city and its founder was the reference to gold. So far, he and Walrus had been focused on the missing diamonds. But those diamonds had been extracted from gold settings. The diamonds, and the other precious stones, had come from heirloom rings, bracelets, pendants and earrings. Where was that gold? Was there a clue to the missing diamonds in the fate of the gold? Maybe, just maybe, there was a link between how the diamonds disappeared and what happened to their gold settings. Since he had nothing else, it was worth an investigation.

CHAPTER 14

Noonan recognized Attucks Musa as a nurk. Nurk, from the old English, was the runt of the litter. Even more telling, it was the least appealing of the litter, the last one chosen for the simple reason it had no redeeming characteristics to make it desirable. Attucks was not ugly or average looking and his body was not too fat or too thin. Facially, he was a seven or an eight. Even more attractive to the opposite sex, he was reasonably heir to an impressive fortune. He had three half-siblings, all of whom had gone on to speckled careers in crime, chemical experimentation and planned anonymity. His brother would not be out of a New York penal institution before the start of the next century, one sister had mentally migrated from LALA Land to a distant planet whose name only she could pronounce and the other sister had forsaken the family, its money and connections and vanished into the megalopolis of Los Angeles. She had had no contact with other members of his family since the last century. His mother, Kankan's sister, and her two husbands, both former, were angling for a share of the inheritance. It was one big, happy family in Micheaux, which, Noonan guessed, made life miserable for Attucks. But then again, he was making life miserable for them as well.

It took Noonan all of one response to understand why Attucks was *persona non grata* in the city of Micheaux family. "Whatever those scum-sucking pigs said about me was a lie and if Aiden had stayed out of Fiona pants, he'd still be married to my mother and if Jasper wasn't such a fruit fly, he'd have had a better marriage – not that my mother is much of a catch. More like the last bitch on the auction block."

"You don't have a lot of nice things to see about your family," Noonan said casually humorously.

Attucks did not pick up the subtle humor.

"Human slimes. All three of them. The kind of people who would be burned at the stake in better times. Protected by my uncle for years, only God knows why."

"Well, be that what it may," Noonan clicked to professional since casual was not working with Attucks. "As I understand Micheaux, you're the man who makes things happen."

Attucks gave Noonan a hard look. "Listen, copper. I know why you're here. I had to talk with the Walrus. I'm to be helpful. Well, I will be. But those diamonds were in their envelopes when they left the bank vault here in Micheaux. I know that because Ambrose what's-his-name, verified the diamonds were in their envelopes. He examined the diamonds. He closed the drawers. I locked the cabinet and off it went with the armored car. What more can I say?"

Whenever Noonan had a disgruntled witness, he went oblique. This was certainly a moment for the technique.

"Before he became Kankan Musa, your uncle was James Clarkson. Were you a Clarkson when you changed your name?"

"You mean, what was my slave name? The name of owners of my great-great-great-grandparents."

"If that's the way you want to put it."

"I do. I'm black and I'm proud. I'm an African-American."

"If you were born here, you're an American."

"I came from African stock."

"I've got German blood but I was born here. That makes me an American. If you don't want to answer, that's fine with me. I'm just looking for background."

Now Attucks went oblique. "March 5, 1770."

"Quite a while back."

"You wanted an answer, I'm giving it to you."

"Fine."

"March 5, 1770, a British soldier went into a tavern to find part-time work. The British did not pay their soldiers well so a lot of their soldiers looked for part-time work."

"I did not know that." Noonan was always willing to learn from history.

"Americans were furious at the British. Money, Cop, money. It's always about money. the French and Indian War was over and now the Americans were paying taxes to cover the cost of the war. But the taxes being collected in the colonies were being used to pay for the Seven Years' War in Europe. American tax dollars should have been fixing up America, not being sent to England. Worse, a lot of British soldiers were in the colonies and they were all looking for part-time work. They were in competition with Americans for every job, part-time and full time."

Noonan was clearly confused. "Why are you telling me this?"

"My story. You asked a question, I'm giving you an answer."

"Go on."

"Well, this British soldier walked into this tavern looking for a part-time job. Pissed the men in the tavern off big time. They chased the British soldier out of the tavern and down the street yelling all kinds of insults at him. He made it to the armory and a lot of British soldiers came out to face the mob. They had weapons, the men from the tavern didn't. At the front of the mob was this tall man, six foot two in an age when most men were five six or five seven. This tall man from the tavern swung a stick at the Captain of the British soldiers and then grabbed the bayonet on one of the soldier's rifle."

Noonan expressed surprise. "Grabbing a bayonet is not a smart idea."

Attucks continued. "History. That's the way it was. The soldier was able to get his gun free and shot the man who had been holding the bayonet. Shot twice. Killed him. Then there was a lot of shooting. That man, the man who grabbed the bayonet, is considered the first man to die for American independence."

"I see. And the point of this story …" Noonan let the sentence hang.

Attucks almost sneered as he leaned toward Noonan. "That man was black. The first man to die for American independence was black. His name was Crispus Attucks. Attucks, his last name, my first one."

Noonan smiled. "Interesting history. But my question was not your first name but your last name."

"No, my last name was not Clarkson. It was Remboldt. My mother, Elizabeth Remboldt, is Kankan's sister. Kankan is my uncle. When he established Micheaux, he asked me to come and work for him. He trusted me. I was right out of college and had no options. No one hired blacks in those days."

"What days were those?"

"1973. When I got here."

"Those were the early days of Affirmative Action. Blacks were being hired all over the United States."

"Maybe, but not for me. Uncle Kankan offered me a good job at good pay so I took it. I've been here ever since."

Noonan opened up his notebook. "I write down everything I hear," he said. "Now, I've been told you pretty much run the town. Even ran it when Kankan Musa was alive."

Attucks smiled. "Ab-so-lu-t-ly. I'm a nuts-and-bolts person. It's not that I have my finger in every pie. I've got to make sure every pie is properly made. I'm not a supervisor in the sense I have to hover over all the action. I find quality people and let them do their job."

"Ever fire anyone?"

Attucks laughed. "All the time. But only those who need to be fired. But I have never fired anyone for what you city people call 'political reasons.' I don't care about politics, as in elected politics. Think of Micheaux as a sophisticated machine. All of the parts and functions have to be mesh. We are not like a big city where you have a choice of, oh, janitorial services, protections services, delivery services. We are all of those. All businesses here service the city buildings and services and those who live here."

"You said protection services. Do you have a police force?"

"Not the way you mean it. We have a few people who handle 'problems,'" Attucks said and made quote marks in the air when he said 'problems.' "When it comes to the things you call felonies, we send for Walrus."

"So," Noonan said as he kept writing, "things like drunk driving, domestic violence, underage drinking, possessing marijuana, and other low level misdemeanors, you handle them by yourself."

"Captain," Attucks said as he shook his head. "We have problems like every other community in America. We just deal with them the way all small towns do. When we have **big** problems, we call in assistance. Other than that, we handle our own."

"I see," said Noonan, still writing. "Now, step by step. Let me tell you what I think happened and you tell me when I go wrong."

"Shoot."

Noonan gave Attucks with an avuncular smile. "Here were go. Since Kankan formed Micheaux City, one of his hobbies was collecting heirloom jewelry."

"He wasn't a collector. He was an investor. He knew the price of gold would go up. Precious stones too. It was a side investment, so to speak. But it wasn't a hobby."

Noonan wrote that down. "OK, so he collected heirlooms over a long period of time. Where did he keep the heirlooms when he collected them?"

"Initially in his home. Where I live now. And, no, there is no wall safe or anything like that. It was an old farm house. About three miles out of town."

"Not in the bank intown?"

Attucks shook his head to indicated Noonan did not understand. "You have to understand, when Combine – that was the name of the city before it was Micheaux – was a city it was just a collection of buildings. It was the center of a farming community. It had a bank, grocery store, tavern, Odd Fellows hall and some smaller structures. Kankan expanded the bank and grocery store. The tavern is now our computer hub for the city and the Odd Fellows hall was upgraded to a hospital. The rest of the structures you see here in town were built as we needed them. Since 1975 or 1976. There were some homes in the vicinity, but not in town. Kankan lived in one. It's three miles outside of Micheaux."

"So," Noonan said, "he kept the heirlooms in his home until when?"

"I'd say about 2005. I don't remember exactly when he brought them to town or why. He never told me. Or anyone else as far as I know. One day he told me that heirlooms were in a deposit box in the bank vault and he wanted to start liquidating them. That was his term, 'liquidating.'"

"Did you see the heirlooms as he collected them?"

"Nope. I didn't really know what kind of value was wrapped up in the heirlooms until he got sick. Then we had to do an inventory of his holdings. That's when I discovered the heirlooms."

"So you did the inventory?"

Attucks gave Noonan a hard look. "I and some lawyers from Sioux Falls did the inventory. It was an extended process. His wealth includes land, buildings, stocks, bonds, real estate in Sioux Falls and odds and ends like the heirlooms."

"What do you mean by 'odds and ends?'"

"Oh, paintings, pieces of artwork, antique furniture. Kankan was not into living high. He was into investing in all kinds of different things. He cooked his own meals, wore pretty much the same clothing year in and year out. His linen closet has sheets and pillow cases from the ice age."

Noonan chuckled. "OK, the heirlooms. They were in a safety deposit box in the vault. When was the decision made to liquidate them?"

"In Kankan's will. He stated, in writing, that his assets should go for the benefit of the City of Micheaux. He wanted all of the buildings he owned to be sold for the benefit of the city. He left his land outside of Micheaux to the Unitarian Church in Sioux Falls and his artwork to a museum to be created in Micheaux."

"Is the museum standing?"

"Not yet."

"And the heirlooms?"

"He stated they were to be liquidated and the money to go for the benefit of the city."

"Why not sell the heirlooms whole, as in rings, pendants, etc."

Attucks smiled sadly. "Captain, to start with, if you sell heirlooms you first have to pay for an appraiser. They are not cheap. And if that appraiser has to come in from Sioux Falls, it's added expense on top of that. Then, if they are auctioned off or sold in an antique store, there is a hefty percentage for the service. We, that is, the probate lawyer and I, checked the provenances … Do you know what a provenance is?"

Noonan nodded. "A written record of who owned the item, when it was bought, how much was paid, that kind of information."

"Correct. Well, many of the heirlooms did not have provenances. Those that did were simply bills of sale. We are not talking about gems the size of the Hope Diamond."

"So the decision was made to separate the gems from the gold and silver. Who made that decision?"

"I suggested it. Kankan approved. I did some research and took a few classes in jewelry. Specifically to learn how to extract precious gems from gold and silver settings. The value of the precious stones and the gold were worth more individually than the heirlooms as units. As I learned, the damage to precious stones was not in the extraction from heirloom but the insertion of the gems into the new pieces of jewelry. The damage to the gold and silver bases is irrelevant because the gold and silver will be melted down and sold for its weight."

Noonan cautiously asked, "Are the gold and silver bases still here in Micheaux?"

Attucks shook his head. "Captain, the extraction of the precious stones took a long time. As the stones were extracted the gold and silver bodies, the settings, were sent to a precious metals operation in Sioux Falls. They are long gone. We have pictures, and photographs of the heirlooms but the bodies, so to speak are gone. We still have provenances, bills of sales, but not the bodies."

Noonan took a moment to write in his notebook. "Now, after a diamond was extracted, what did you do with the diamond."

"Don't you read police reports?"

"Humor me. I'm here and the reports are who knows where."

Attucks sneered. "Cops! OK, as each diamond was extracted, that's the professional term, 'extracted,'" he made quote marks again in the air. "As each gem was extracted it was put in the industry-accepted envelopes. Every envelope had a code which linked it back with the heirloom from which it had come. I'm an amateur jeweler. By that I mean I know enough about gems from my classes, to make an estimate of the size of the gem. Value, I don't guess. That's why we, I, contracted with Brody and Sons. They're out of Sioux Falls but have connections in New York. They recommended getting the batch GemPrinted for security purposes."

"Why?" Noonan asked. "That would just be an added cost."

"True. We could try to sell the gems on the market as heirlooms. But with so many there would be suspicion. If we sold them one at a time, yes, we could make money but that would take time and a lot of trips to New York. We were into the money, to use a 1960s expression, not the effort. GemPrinting was a good option. The cost per gem was low but we would make up for that cost by the quickness that the gems would sell. With GemPrints, Brody and Sons could sell the diamonds anywhere in any number with no one being suspicious as to where they came from. Remember, if a gem is discovered to be stolen, the cops seize the gem. The buyer is out the cost of the gem and the gem itself. Yes, a GemPrint per stone was a cost, but with a GemPrint no one is going to worry that stone had been stolen."

Noonan looked at his notes and said, "Well, so the writing on each envelope was just, say, a number and that number linked back to the heirloom it had come from."

"Correct. My writing, that is. Then, when Ambrose Brody examined a gem, he put the size of the gem on the envelope. He was the pro and he was going to have to sell it."

"So he went stone by stone."

"Correct."

"And he never saw the rings and pendants and whatever bodies, the settings?"

"No, he asked to see a few of them. I suspect he wanted to make sure the gems came from heirlooms."

"You showed him the heirlooms?"

"I showed him the ones that had not been sent to Sioux Falls. He matched some gems in envelopes with the pieces of jewelry we still had to make sure the numbering was accurate."

"Was it?"

"Yup. I did it myself."

"OK, then Ambrose Brody sat at a table and went through the gems one at a time."

"Correct."

"In the vault?"

"Correct. I set up a special table for him."

"You saw him examine each stone?"

"Correct. I know what you are thinking and the answer is 'no.' He rolled each gem, one at a time, out of the envelope, examined it with a loop and handed it to me. I put it back in its envelope and put the envelope back in the tray of gems. Could he have switched some stones while I wasn't looking? Sure, but not 63 stones."

"So you saw him examine all the gems, one at a time, and put each one of them back in their individual envelopes."

"Every one. Then I locked the drawers, three of them, and then locked the cabinet."

"Then both of you left the vault."

"When was the vault opened again?"

"Later that night. We had an organ donor here in Micheaux. Gave a kidney. It had to be in Omaha the next day. So the vault was opened and the kidney put in."

"The security footage for the armored car shows the people in heavy over jackets. Was the vault refrigerated."

"Yes. Doctor's orders. We had not had an organ donation like this one so we did what the doctor ordered."

"Why was the organ taken by armored car. I would have assumed that organs would be taken by plane. More speedy."

"True. It was a black thing. You, being white, wouldn't understand."

"Educate me."

"The man donating the kidney, and I cannot tell you his name, was a long-time, African-American resident. Personal friend of Kankan. He helped build the city. Was one of the founders of Micheaux Transport and Delivery. His nephew needed a kidney in Omaha. Sending the kidney by plane meant paying someone outside of Micheaux for the transportation.

Using Micheaux Transport and Delivery meant the money stayed here in Micheaux. The doctor in Omaha said 'fine,' just make it quick. Kidney went into the vault at about11 p.m. and was out at 6 a.m. the next morning. Arrived in Omaha in time for the transplant."

"So you went into the vault with the kidney and then came out?"

"In and out."

"How long were you in the vault?"

"A few minutes."

"That's what the security footage will show?"

"Hope so. It will show me going in with an organ transport container and coming out without a box."

"Why did it take you several minutes to take the organ in and get out?"

"I had to make sure the room was cold enough. The doctors, both of them, in Micheaux and Omaha, gave me specific instructions as to the temperature of the vault. I had to make sure the vault temperature was accurate. It took me that long to make sure the temperature was set correctly – and operating correctly. It had to be quite cold."

"And you came out with nothing?"

"Look at the security tapes for yourself."

CHAPTER 15

Doctor Hazleton Fitzsimons was as black as the Ace of Spades. And he was sensitive to his color. "Just because I'm black does not mean I'm less than competent."

"I never said that," Noonan said. "As long as you were approved by the State of South Dakota Medical Board, you're competent."

"Not everyone thinks that way."

"I do," Noonan said as he pulled out his notebooks. "That's all that matters now."

"Nice to hear it. For a starter, I know nothing about the missing diamonds and I have already talked to every law enforcement and insurance person AND their brothers."

"Then it'll be easy for me." Noonan smiled. "Just a rundown on the kidney transplant."

"Simple. The patient, and I cannot tell you his name, donated a kidney to a nephew, whose name I also cannot give you. The patient was here and the recipient was in Omaha. The patient was – and is, he's still alive – a long-term resident of Micheaux. One of the originals. We, the latecomers are called the dozens. Not originals."

"How many of the 'originals' are left?"

"Less than a handful. Only one is young, so to speak. Attucks. He came right of college because his uncle, Kankan, hired him. The rest were Kankan's age. Kankan died at 73, two years ago. The patient in question is three years older."

"In good health now that a kidney has been removed?"

"He has great genes. He'll be around for another three decades."

Noonan looked at his notebook. "So, he demanded that the kidney, his kidney, go by armored car?"

"Yup. He made the arrangement with Attucks. It was not a sudden decision."

"Organ transplants are usually arranged by the doctor of the recipient, right?"

"Yes. I'd say in almost all cases. The time for the transplant for this particular patient was scheduled as it was for a reason I cannot mention."

Noonan thought for a moment and then said, "Like, perhaps, the recipient was in jail and the State of South Dakota was not willing to pay for a transplant?"

"I didn't say that," Fitzsimons said.

Noonan did a mmm and then said, "Once this recipient was in a location where the transplant could take place, then it was scheduled. Would that be an accurate statement?"

"Yes. Assuming you do not have a medical background …."

"Which I do not," replied Noonan.

Fitzsimons continued, "Keeping this as simple as possible, when it comes to a transplant there are four issues which have to come together at precisely the same time. The recipient has to be needy enough for the transplant. The recipient has been strong enough for the transplant. A donor has to available. The DNA of the donor and the recipient have to be close enough for the transplant to be possible."

"Which," Noonan said as he scribbled in his notebook, "with the donor an uncle that would make the match reasonable."

"A medical gift of the gods," Fitzsimons said. "And in the medical profession, we do not trust to gods."

"I see," Noonan replied. "That's three of the four requirements."

"Correct. The fourth is the speed of the organ from donor to recipient. Faster is better."

"And in this case?" Noonan asked.

"This was an unusual case. First, because it was the first transplant recipient I had dealt with. Ten years ago, we here in Micheaux would not have had the ability to do the extraction. Compared to now, the hospital was in the dark ages. Today, well, it's a different story."

"How about second and third?"

"Second, the kidney was going to go by armored car. I would have preferred the kidney to go by plane but there were complications. Money was a big one. Organ delivery by plane is often free but only if there is a plane available. There wasn't."

"How far ahead of time did you and the recipient and the donor know a transplant would take place?"

"A month. Maybe six weeks. There were many factors beyond our control."

"How long between the time you knew the organ could be removed and the actual removal?"

"There is no simple answer to that question. If a patient is ready on Monday that does not mean the transplant can take place in the next 24 hours. There are other issues. Like is a transplant doctor available? Is a hospital available that can schedule the transplant? When can the donor donate the kidney? Is there a hospital available for the kidney to be removed? Is transportation available for the kidney to be transported. You are a cop and you want yes-and-no answers to questions which cannot be answered with a 'yes' or a 'no.' Whatever I say it sounds like I'm lying."

Noonan chuckled. "OK, let me ask the question another way. When all of the pieces for the transplant were in place, how long was that before the kidney was removed?"

"About a week."

"So everyone knew a week ahead of time, the kidney was going to be transferred."

"Y-e-s-s, but like I said, there are a lot of extraneous factors involved."

"I understand," Noonan said. "But everyone involved knew when the kidney was going to be removed."

"Correct."

"And everyone knew the kidney was going by armored car, not a plane."

"Correct. That's what the patient wanted and he was paying for the whole operation, his and his nephew's. Ooops, I didn't say 'nephew.'"

"I didn't hear that," Noonan chuckled. "But you talked with the patient here before the extraction?"

"Yes."

"Did he tell you he wanted the kidney to move by armored car?"

"He didn't say anything about the transportation of the kidney. He was the perfect patient. All he wanted was a guarantee that his kidney was going to his nephew and not to someone else."

"How did you guarantee that?"

"I showed him the paperwork with his, er, the recipient's name."

"That satisfied him?"

"That's all he asked. Then he went under."

"Under? As in when the operation began?"

"Correct."

"How long did the operation take?"

"Not long. Under an hour. Removal of an organ is not lengthy. It's the insertion that takes the time."

"OK. Now, once the organ has been extracted, what happens to it?"

"It is placed in a sterilized environment. In this case, a surgical bag, if you will. Ice is placed around the bag and then the ice and surgical bag are sealed in a transport crate. Then the crate is given to the transport company, in this case Micheaux Transport and Delivery."

"But it did not leave Micheaux immediately."

"Correct. The out-of-town delivery was with the diamonds everyone is asking about. The removal of the kidney finished at about 11 in the evening. The armored car was to leave about six the next morning."

"Did you instruct the armored car people to keep the box refrigerated?"

"Oh, yes. It does not make any sense to put a refrigerated box in a hothouse and expect the organ to be unaffected."

"Assuming the crate retained its refrigeration and the transport was in a refrigerated environment, how long would the kidney be viable, if that's the correct term?"

"Viable is correct enough. Kidneys are the more resilient of all organs. Once harvested, our medical term, they are viable for as long as 36 hours. But the faster they are transplanted, to use a term you would understand, faster is better."

"And refrigeration is necessary?"

"Absolutely."

CHAPTER 16

Attucks was no less amiable when Noonan cornered him again.
"What? Again? What did I leave out?"

"You answered all my questions, Attucks. I just have a few more."

"Well, make it quick."

"Three questions. First, when the insurance company pays for the missing diamonds, who gets the money?"

"The city of Micheaux. We are going to use the money to incorporate. I guess you'd say the money will be spent the way the new city councils want it spent. But that's a ways down the road."

"OK, Question Number Two. The three who were in the Micheaux Transport and Delivery with the gems and the organs. Harriet Albertson, Daniel Sandusky and Juliette Musa. Do you get along with them?"

Attucks laughed. "Hardly." He snorted. "They have been impossible to work with."

"Impossible? As in you do not get along with them or they are not to be trusted."

"Trusted?! Seriously! If it weren't for fear of the hoosegow, they'd have driven off with a loaded armored car years ago. Crooked? When they die the undertaken won't have to use a shovel. He'll just screw them into the ground."

"So, they have stolen something in the past?"

"Not yet. Not the brains or the balls."

"How about you, since we are talking about honesty."

"I'm walking in a dead man's shoes."

"I'm not familiar with the term."

"Means I'm going to benefit from all of Uncle Kankan's estate. I may not get actual ownership but I will still be paid for all the work I am dong here. To keep my job, jobs actually, all I have to do is keep doing what I am doing the keep my nose clean."

"You seem pretty sure of yourself?"

"Sure! Absolutely! I'm the only one who can do it! I have been groomed for it. I've worked in all Kankan's businesses here in Micheaux. Bottom to top. Armored car, museum, confetti production line, bank, real estate office. You may not think much of my attitude, for which I don't give . . ."

Noonan cut off the end of the sentence. "I get your point. Now, to my point, I'll be blunt. As I understand, there are three armored car drivers. You don't like them and, I'm guessing, they do not like you."

"I have to work with them. I don't trust them. That's why I am the only one to handle the cash and valuables. They handle pick and delivery. Nothing else."

"You don't trust them with cash?"

"They would steal a red-hot stove."

"Well, if you pick up the cash. What do they pick up?"

"Everything else. Don't think of the armored car business as just picking up money. We pick up valuables, documents, paintings and other stuff like that. We weekly pickups from the mines in the area. I'll bet you didn't know this part of South Dakota is loaded with mines. Big and small. There are regular pickups of the gold. That's what Micheaux Transport and Delivery does most of the time. It's safe. I mean, the gold is safe. It's inventoried to the gram at the mines and then transferred to the bank. The Micheaux Bank. My uncle's bank. Paperwork at both ends. No way to skim a few bucks. Once every so often the gold from the bank vault goes to this refinery or that refinery. Again, paperwork in and paperwork out. No chance for the armored car staff to skim."

"I'm not interested in the gold, Attucks. I'm interested in the diamonds. They are the items that are missing."

"Well, they're not here. The feds checked every security deposit box in the vault. The feds checked the ventilation system and the bathroom and my home. They checked a lot of building in town. Yes, the diamonds are gone. The insurance company will pay the city. I'm not in the loop for any cash. That should finish your questions."

Noonan chuckled. "Until the diamonds are found, everyone's a suspect. You should know that. I just want to know if it were possible for the three Micheaux Transport and Delivery people to have gotten sticky fingers."

"With the collective IQ of a cloud of jellyfish? Unlikely. They go into the bank vault to drop off the gold shipments and then leave the vault. They are only in the vault and safety deposit area for, at the most, say a minute. Not enough time to break into a safety deposit box. Besides, to get into a safety deposit box you'd have to have the key for the individual box as well as the passkey. Even if they could somehow find where my uncle's diamonds they'd need a passkey to get into the cabinet. I have one passkey. There is one in Omaha where the rubies and sapphires were unloaded and the last one is with the GemPrint folks in Kansas City. The armored car folks could not steal anything."

"How about you?"

"Ha! Typical cop question. First, I'd have the same problem getting the gems as those three delivery people. Even more important, I don't go into the vault for very long whenever I go in. Even more important. Why should I steal something that is basically mine? Now that Uncle Kankan is gone and I'm in his will as the executor of all of his property not deeded to someone. Why should I steal anything?"

"What about your mother? Kankan's sister. Isn't she in the mix? I mean for an inheritance."

"Lizzy the Lezzie. My mother. My birth father died years ago. My mother's been remarried twice since then. She and my two step-fathers have been fighting tooth, nail, bankbook and claw since the day she was married, both times. This is a small town and they are always running into each other. They all have their own friends, his, his and hers, gay, straight and polywhatever and whomever. All the three have in common is fighting."

"So, they have filed for divorce, your mother and step-fathers?"

"A while back. Both my step-dads worked for mom. It's never pleasant being around any of them. Both of my step-fathers have trusts from when they were bought out of my mom's businesses. She's been successful in spite of them. They, both of 'em, are leaches. None of us are close."

Attucks gave Noonan a suspicious look. "And before you ask, no, I will not a get a dime of Kankan's money. I am the executor of the Kankan estate, not a recipient of any of the moneys or property. All his property and money will go for what he intended, the benefit of the city. So I will not get a dime of the money from the gold or silver or gems or diamonds even though I am responsible for paying for the conversion and," Attucks said snidely, "all of the pain and agony of this ongoing investigation of disappearing diamonds."

CHAPTER 17

"A real piece of work, that Attucks Musa," Ambrose Brody said flatly. "Pure as the driven snow."

"Was he difficult to work with?" Noonan asked.

Brody and Noonan were sitting in Brody and Sons' office in Sioux Falls. Noonan had his notebook out and Ambrose was working on a cup of coffee even though it was well after the noon hour.

"Difficult to worth with," Ambrose mused. "Captain, everyone in this business is difficult to work with. The precious gem business is not like any other business on the planet. Let me state it in a way a cop would understand. There are, quite literally, millions of dollars sitting on a table and with any one stone someone could retire. It's not the greedy thieves you have to watch out for. It's the individual who sees a shot at early retirement. One diamond could do it, particularly if the diamond does not have a GemPrint."

"What about if a diamond has a GemPrint?"

"To use an example from your world, a GemPrint is like a fingerprint. When a perpetrator, to use your terms, leaves a fingerprint at the crime scene, the fingerprint is put in a database. If there is a match, you've got your man. Or woman. No match simply means the perpetrator is not in the system. GemPrint is the same. If a diamond with a GemPrint vanishes and no one declares it missing, no one searches for it. If it gets put in a piece of jewelry and sold, it is usually not GemPrinted. The jewelry could pass through ten hands before it is GemPrinted and by then any Statute of Limitations has expired. Sure, the gem gets taken by the cops but no one is charged with the theft."

Noonan smiled. "That's been a long bounce around my question."

Ambrose smiled. "Attucks is no different than any other multi-gem client we have or had. He is, to use to use an old adage, penny wise and pound foolish. When I was going over the precious stones he was watching me like a hawk. There was really no reason to be watching me at all. I did not own the stones and I was not buying the stones. He had the ownership of the stones and the only money Brody and Sons was going to make was a percentage of the sale. Or sales. Sure, I might have been able to snag a diamond or two but not 63. Even if I did snag a diamond or two, when I sold it there would be a paper trail. Then the feds would ask me for the paperwork proving I had acquired the stone legally. Everyone is watching everyone else in the diamond business. There are not a lot of secrets."

"So you didn't snatch a stone?"

"Not a one," Brody said with a laugh. "Besides, I and the office here," he pointed to the BRODY AND SONS sign, "were thoroughly searched."

Noonan chucked. "Was there any particular reason you were in the vault to analyze the precious stones rather than an office in the bank?"

"I was never told one. The Micheaux collection was odd because it was not in a secure, jewelry location. As far as I know, the city does not have a jeweler. Even if the city did have a jeweler, the stones were not in the possession of a jeweler. Was it unusual be in a vault examining stones, not really. Did I find it unusual? Not really."

"Now, I was told that every stone you examined was put in an envelope with numbers already on the envelopes.'

"Correct. I was told the numbers linked to the heirloom jewelry."

"And you saw the heirloom jewelry?"

"A few settings. But the bulk of them were long gone. To a precious metals firm in Sioux Falls. Frankly, I did not care about the settings. I was going to sell the precious stones, not the settings."

"Fair enough," Noonan kept writing in his notebook. "So, stone by stone, you examined the gems and then replaced them in their envelope."

"Correct. But before I replaced them I indicated their carats."

"You actually wrote on each envelope?"

"Yes. I'll tell you the same thing I told the FBI and the insurance people, I examined each stone, one at a time, and wrote its characteristics on the envelope it came in. Then I gave the envelope to Attucks who replaced the envelope in the tray. Then he handed me the next envelope. One at a time."

"Attucks watched you the whole time."

"Like a hawk."

"Was anyone else in the vault with the two of you?"

"Just the two of us."

"How long did the examination and writing on the envelopes take?"

"Over a two-day period, I'd say about six hours."

"And during those six hours no one else came into the vault?"

"No one."

"And Attucks was there the whole time."

"He escorted me in and escorted me out."

Noonan kept scribbling. "Now, when you came back into the vault before the cabinet was picked up by the armored car delivery people, did you examine the stones again?"

"Not the way you mean. I'd say it was procedure rather than suspicion. The tray to the cabinet was opened and I looked at about a dozen precious stones at random. Just to make sure they were there."

"Did you pour them out of the envelopes or just look inside?"

"Just looked inside. On some of them I just squeezed them to make sure there was something inside. No, I did not roll out a stone and examine it with a loop. But, speaking to law enforcement, what difference does that make? All the diamonds were gone. They were in the envelopes when Attucks locked the cabinet. They were not there when the cabinet was opened at the GemPrint facility. Something happened to them along the way."

Noonan thought for a long moment and then asked, "Were you there when the cabinet was loaded into the armored car?"

"Of course, I had been there before the car arrived. That's when I did a cursory examination of the stones. It was there about five in the morning and the armed car people, two women and a man, came at six."

"No chance the drawer with the diamonds was switched when the armored car people came in?"

"Not a chance. I was there. Attucks locked the cabinet. He rolled the cabinet to the vault door and said something like 'come and get it.' Then he indicated a box and the armored car three took it as well."

"Do you know what was in the box?"

"An organ of some kind. There was lettering on the side that said something like 'Organ inside.' That's why the vault was so cold. To keep the organ, what, usable?"

"The vault was cold?"

"Frigid. For the organ. I was happy I didn't have to spend that much time inside."

CHAPTER 18

Walrus was not having a good day. "I hope you have done better than I have."

Noonan chuckled. "What makes you think I have some revelations?"

"Because I don't."

Noonan chuckled. "You've got to have faith, Walrus. Good comes to those with patience."

"Well, I've got no patience."

"Speaking of patients...."

"Yeah, I talked with the transplant doc in Omaha. To use your term, I got zip. The patient, whose name was not revealed," Walrus looked at the ceiling as if say 'why in God's name does that not make a difference.' "All the doctor would tell me was that the patient was black and the kidney had come from a relative."

"How about the operation?"

"A success. Patient is doing well."

"How about the timing?"

"Sort of around and about with the explanation. All he would admit was that the patient had some 'legal issues' that had to be addressed before the operation could place."

"Nothing about the legal issues?"

"Nope. There were lots of blacks being released from incarceration about the time of the operation. No last names Musa or Remboldt. Besides, the operation was legal so there was not a lot I could look into."

"How about the kidney?"

"Doc said it was good and the operation was a success."

"Did you ask about the box the kidney came in?"

"Yup. Apparently the FBI already has it."

"Let me guess, the FBI had said nothing."

"Another zip."

"And nothing on the diamonds showing up?"

"Third time zip."

Noonan kind of squinted. "Well, we have to follow the money. But in this case, there is no money to follow. We know for sure the diamonds were stolen. Tracking them is going to be problem because they have not been GemPrinted."

"I don't know about that," Walrus said. "You know, Heinz, if I had stolen 63 diamonds, I'd want to sell them. Diamonds are not money. But diamonds are worth money. To get money from diamonds you have to sell them. But it would be a chore to sell them one at a time."

"I agree with you," Noonan said. "Let's follow this forward. Whoever stole the diamonds – and however they did it – will have a problem getting money for the diamonds. Is it possible whoever stole the diamonds is going to do an under-the-table deal with Brody and Sons? Maybe take the diamonds out of the country and make the sale?"

Walrus shook his head. "Maybe but I doubt it. I'm sure the FBI is watching Brody and Sons and every move they make. Anything funky and the feds will be on them like white on rice. Tomorrow, next week, a year from now, Brody and Sons is being watched. They are a pretty aboveboard operation. Been in business for two generations. I don't see them being involved."

"How about the insurance company. Maybe they pay 15% to the thieves to get the diamonds back?"

"A possibility but, again, we're not going to know that happened. We might not be able to do anything about it. But at least we'd know the diamonds had been found. And, as of this moment, we don't know diddly."

"Well," Noonan said with a smile, "let's talk to someone who does know diddly."

"Like whom?"

"The insurance company. They have the most to lose."

"Right," said Walrus as he stood up to put on a jacket. "Just what a need. To be lied to by a professional!"

CHAPTER 19

Hortensia Rodrigues, agent for Rodrigues LLC of Sioux Falls, would have made the perfect Prisoner of War during World War II. All she knew for sure was her name, rank and serial number – and she stated she did not have a rank or serial number. She said everything to be said had been said to the police and there was nothing to add. Walrus said he was the police and Rodrigues, again, repeated her name, rank and serial number – and then stated she did not have a rank or serial number.

CHAPTER 20

"I'm getting used to your term 'zip', Heinz. This case has been nothing more than one zip after another."

Noonan smiled. "True. This case is only different inthat we can't go back to the first step because there is none."

"No scene of the crime, peachy. And there's no way to follow the money because right now, there is none."

"Actually," Noonan said as he fiddled with his notebook, "there is a way to follow money that does not exist."

"Do tell."

"Let's look at this crime backward."

"Backwards?"

"Right. We've been concentrating on what happened to the diamonds. Let's focus on what will happen if the diamonds are not recovered."

"Ouch!"

"Don't 'ouch!' yet. We are a long way from losing this one. Now, let's just suppose we cannot find the diamonds. What will happen to those diamonds?"

Walrus shook his head. "They'll sell them and keep the money."

"True," Noonan tossed his pen in the air and caught it. "Wherever you go to sell a diamond, you are going to have to show ID. I don't know much about the diamond business but I'll bet you will get a check

104

of some kind, not cash. Maybe for a stone or two you could get cash, but not 63 of them. So, to sell the diamonds, you have to receive a check. To cash the check you have to have a bank account."

Walrus chuckled. "I don't see the thief being so stupid as to start a checking account in his or her own name."

"I don't either," Noonan said. "Most likely the check will be made out to a company."

"Well," Walrus stretched. "If it was made out to a company, I doubt the thieves would use their real names. They would want to put at least one person between them and the crime."

"I agree," Noonan started writing. "If I were planning this heist, I would have laid the groundwork long ago. Probably before Kankan died. There is more going on here than just the diamond theft. Let me toss a few ideas around."

"Fine with me."

"Kankan's wealth is in many forms: land, buildings, cash, stocks, bonds and heirlooms. All we have been doing is concentrating on the heirlooms."

"I thought Kankan's will laid out who got what."

"I thought so too," Noonan replied. "But I do not even know if there was a will. If there is no will, who is the executor? More important, what are the restrictions in the will. Attucks said Kankan wanted some buildings to go to the city. But *wanted* is different than *willed*."

"So," Walrus was suddenly alive with curiosity, "what you are saying is that there is a lot more loot on the table than the diamonds."

"Could be. The diamond theft could have been someone getting too greedy."

Walrus shook his head. "Been there, done that."

Noonan fiddled with his notebook. "Let's follow this thought forward. If someone knew the will did not specifically state who got what, that could open a window of opportunity for a disreputable sort."

"Money has a tendency to bring those folks out of the woodwork."

"True. Step one would be to be in a position to take advantage of the old man."

"That's a no-brainer. Attucks."

"My guess too. But let's not convict him yet. We have to see what the will states."

"So we have to get a copy of the will."

"Step one. Step two is see who the executor is."

"My guess, again. Attucks."

"My bet too. But," Noonan held up a cautionary finger, "unless Attucks is specifically identified as the person to receive such and such property, he does not get it outright."

"If he is the executor, can he give it to himself?"

"Maybe. I'm not a lawyer. But since there is squabbling over the will, I'd say he can't take it outright. If he wants to take the land and buildings and whatever else that is not specifically identified as going to someone, he gets to decide who gets it. If he is smart, he'll figure a way to wash his name from the acquisition. Keep himself arm's length away, legally speaking."

Walrus rolled his eyes. "So he has to find a useful idiot."

"Got it."

Walrus laughed. "Well, there are a lot of idiots in South Dakota. How do we find the useful one Attucks used?"

Noonan shook a finger comically at Walrus. "I'm not ready to say Attucks stole the diamonds. We're a long way from a conviction. As far as Kankan's will and intentions, no laws have been broken. Even if Attucks is the executor."

"Cherries. So he can steal and get away with it!"

"What he could be doing is legal. As far as we know. What is not legal is selling stolen property. I am assuming that the plan to convert Kankan land to cash in his pocket has long been in the making."

"With some useful idiot."

"My guess. Now, hear me out, Walrus. One of three things has happened. Our idiot set up a local business that will receive the property. I doubt this because it would be too easy to ferret out whose hands were dirty. Second, a corporation would be formed. Then the land and building transfer would be to a legal entity. There would be no single name involved."

"But the names of the corporate officers and stock owners would be public knowledge."

"True. Even more important. The corporation and its officers can be sued. So, if the corporation were to *absorb*, shall we say, the land and buildings, disgruntled relatives of Kankan could sue. It would take years to settle."

"OK, what's number three?"

"Number three would be a trust. The executor could transfer the ownership of a piece of property to a trust. There is some legal protection there. A trust cannot be sued. Individuals who have authority over the trust or are part-owners can be sued, but not the trust itself."

Walrus nodded his head. "I know all about trusts because my wife is part of one. From her mother who is still alive. Your three options are informative. I agree that just setting up a business to get the money is out. I don't see anyone who is, shall way say, bent, be willing to trust someone else to take his money with no legal way to make sure he gets the money back. Corporation is a good idea but there are still names involved. But the trust would have names listed as well. If it were me, I'd set up a sham corporation and let the money pass through the corporation into a trust. That would pull me out of the spotlight At least for a while."

Noonan smiled. "Exactly what I was thinking. But I was going one step further. Suppose there was another step. A legal one. Suppose the scenario is as you have said. But in the last step, the property is deeded out of the trust to someone. There will no record of that transaction. There will just be property transfer documents filed with the State of South Dakota. That document will not appear in the corporation records."

"If it was deeded to an individual. If it went to another corporation it would be listed that way."

"True," Noonan mused. "But if I was a clever criminal, I'd have the trust transfer to a corporation in another state. Then the ownership of the land registered with the State of South Dakota would list the corporation as the owner, not the executor."

"This is all fine and dandy," Walrus said as he scratched his head. "But everything so far is legal. And why would anyone let this guy just walk away with all the property? The other people in the corporations, all of them, have to be making something out of the deal or it is back to court and probate for a century."

"True. And if I were doing it I would string the properties through one at time to keep people from getting greedy."

"But where does this get us? This would all be just a shuffling of ownership of property that is legal."

"Where we could be getting is the diamonds. Whoever sells them is going to have to have some ID. And payment for the diamonds will have to be by check. If the scenario we just finished is in place, the check for the diamonds will be to a corporation."

Walrus shook his head. "I can see people getting involved in land transfers that are legal. Stealing and selling diamonds is a whole other ball game."

"I agree. For us, it's a matter of tracing the syzygy. Are you familiar with the term?"

"Uh, no."

"It's an astronomical term. It's where three or more planets line up. When two things line it, it's an alignment. More than two, syzygy. One of the few words in the English language that does not have a vowel."

"I'll remember that. How does a syzygy apply to this case?"

"Whoever is the mastermind, that person is not in this alone. Forget the land and buildings for the moment. Whatever happens to them can be traced with documents. But the diamonds are another matter altogether. For anyone to get away with the diamonds, there are a lot of things they will have to do. And those things have come in order. They have to hide the diamonds until the heat is off. Then they have to transport the diamonds to where they can sell them. They will have to make every sale legal. Then they will have to wash the money. Then they will have to divide the money."

"That's why we follow the money."

Noonan shook his head slowly. "Y-e-s-s, but from where we are sitting, this case will get very dicey very quickly. If I were a betting man – which I am not – I would say the thief already has a second laundering system set up. He'll – or she'll – use a fake identification to sell the stones. Probably one or two at a time in different cities. Since the stones have not been GemPrinted, there will be no alarm bells when the stones are checked to make sure they were not stolen. Then the purchase checks will be written to the corporation. The corporation could then transfer the money to a trust. As long as the corporation pays the income taxes, no one will be the wiser."

Noonan smiled. "And if the trust transfers the money to a bank in Switzerland, it just," popped the fingers of his right hand, "vanishes."

Walrus shook his head. "No taxes, no paper trail, no perp."

Noonan said. "Very clever. Whoever pulled this off was thinking long-term. My bet, he has a double set of books, so to speak. He has the main one that will receive the property. That one will be easy to find. The second one, where he walks away with the money from the diamonds will be hard to find."

"But we are going to have to find it fast," Walrus said shaking his head. "Once this case goes cold, it will only a matter of a month or two before our bird flies."

"I agree," Noonan now began writing in his notebook. "I'd like to suggest we split up the responsibilities. I need to go back to Micheaux and look around, talk to some folks I didn't believe were involved before."

"Fine with me, what do you want me to do?"

"Several things. First, take every name of everyone I, you, the FBI and the insurance company talked to. Run their names through the corporation databases for South Dakota, Kansas and Missouri. Do the same for trusts. There might be a national database as well. Then pull up all the new drivers' licenses for South Dakota for the past year, men and women. See if you can find death certificates which match. I'm inclined to believe a woman is involved."

"That's sexist. Why?"

"If a man wants a new driver's license, he'd better have a good reason and more than just a birth certificate. A woman can claim she was married in another state and then went through a bitter divorce. That's why the name on the birth certificate she stole could be different from the name she wants the new ID to show. She can get a South Dakota ID easily. Then she can come back for a driver's license later."

"And it will give us a residence address."

"Yup," replied Noonan. "And if our perps are clever, they've already sent letters to the fake woman's supposed residence and possibly paid for some utilities in her name."

"You're thinking like a cop."

"There's a good reason for that!" Noonan chuckled. "While I am off and away in Micheaux, I have another task for you. It will take some finesse because you will be dealing with the FBI."

"Oh, goody, goody."

"See if you can get a copy of Kankan's will. Technically it is not an aspect of the crime. But you never know. I don't see Attucks giving us a copy. I'll bet the FBI has a copy. See if you can sweet talk the Gmen into giving you a copy. Or at least reading it."

Walrus shook his head. "A fool's errand, I'm afraid, but I'm on it. I'm betting our perp is miles ahead of us."

Noonan smiled. "Yes, but we are traveling at the speed of light."

CHAPTER 21

If there was any one thing Noonan knew, in the real world there was a substantial difference between bright and smart. Stated as simply as possible, if you finish your homework, you are bright. When you turn it in you are smart. Bright has no value if you are not smart. Anyone can be smart. All it takes is a brain and everyone has one of those. Most people do not use the brain they have but, at both the beginning and end of the day, all people do have an organ called a brain. But your brain only has value if it is used. Every day of every person's life, he or she, inputs information. The more input you have, the smarter and brighter you become. People who read add substantially more information faster. As Noonan always told his twin boys, "Not every book is a good one but every good one will change your life."

When it comes to criminals, the gap between bright and smart is Grand Canyonesque. Noonan had seen far more than his fair share of bright criminals. But the smart ones were very few. The smartest felons had multiple scenarios. If Plan A appears to be in doubt, Plan B switches into gear. Thereafter, there is a Plan C and Plan D. Even if all goes well, there are long term disasters that must be dodged. There is a forensic evidence left at the crime scene, the persistence of the FBI along with the ongoing, yearly, nitpicking scrutiny of the IRS. Noonan, an historian at heart, wholeheartedly believed in the Greek god Atë.

She was the god of mischief, delusion and blind folly which leads men down the path of ruin.

Crime only paid in very few cases and in most of those cases, the criminals were lawyers. In every case there are things you could prove and things you know but cannot not prove. The key to being a successful detective of crime was moving the things you could not prove into the column of those you can. Prosecutors did not care what you think. If you did not have the evidence, you had nothing.

It was not going to be possible to look at Kankan Musa's will. It had nothing to do with the theft of the diamonds and even a first-year law student could stop that in court. So, for the moment, there were no documents to examine. When there are no documents, concentrate on people.

So it was back to Micheaux.

CHAPTER 22

Noonan had never seen a photograph of Kankan Musa so, because of his focus on black ethnicity, Noonan expected him to be quite dark. He was therefore quite surprised to find his sister, Elizabeth so light she could pass for white. And she was not what he had expected. Living in a rural setting like Micheaux, he expected to find, at the very least, a woman dressed in ranch work clothes. She was not. She was dressed for corporate success. Not as a secretary or office manager but as a business owner. She was through-and-through business – and corporate business at that, not half of a mom-and-pop.

"You're that Sherlock Holmes guy, right?"

"I've been lucky."

"Then you're the **Sheer** Luck Holmes." It was said with a tinge of humor.

"Works for me. You are Kankan's sister?"

She gave him the corporate, been-there-done-that look. "Yes. I know. You were expecting Aunt Jemimah."

"No, I was expecting Elizabeth Remboldt."

"That was me. Once upon a time. Before that it was Clarkson. Now it's Reynolds. I am sure that," and she gave a long pause before she continued, "son" stated as though she were spitting, "told you all about my personal life."

Noonan was law and order bland. "It never came up. As long as you know why I'm here, I've got some questions to ask."

"Ask away. I don't have the diamonds."

"You know where they are?"

"The rings of Saturn. I'll tell you the same thing I told everyone else with a badge. My son and I are, in a word from your world, estranged. He lives in his world, I have mine."

Noonan smiled and pulled out a notebook. "I won't take much of your time."

"I'm sure you want to look around the place too. Fine with me. You won't need a warrant because one's already been issued. So come one on in and ask away."

Contrary to what he expected to find, the interior of the Reynolds home was more office than a residence. She waved him into an empty chair. Beside a desk with piles of paper neatly stacked in four or five piles. "Let me save you some time and casual, around the bush, questions. Kankan and I grew up middle class. We both went to college. He got a degree in history and became a teacher. My degree was in business administration. He was a lot more successful than I was. He knew where to find money; I just knew how to manage it. In the early days, he needed me to keep an eye on his investments. That's why I came to Micheaux."

"Well," said Noonan looking around. "You appear to be successful."

"I'd have been a lot more successful if I had stayed single," she chortled. "Right now I'm managing five businesses." She swept her hands over the pile of papers. "I don't own any of the businesses, the bank does. But I'm the only shareholder. Five LLCs."

"I'm impressed," Noonan said truthfully.

"Being black has not helped. Being the sister of Kankan hasn't helped. Being married twice hasn't helped. Working hard and taking risks has. So, before you ask, I run a hunting operation with a remote lodge about 60 miles from here. I own, that is, the bank and I own a small flight service with a mail contract. That's how I reach the hunting lodge. I maintain a small slaughterhouse for the game animals during the hunting season and local livestock the rest of the year. The other businesses are a lot smaller, a temp agency and a local art investment operation. I need the temp agency because the lodge is not open year-round and frankly, I don't like the idea of hiring locals for four months and then forcing them to live on welfare for the other eight. If you work for me, you will work fulltime but not at the same job the whole time."

"I'm impressed."

"Don't be. If America expects to stay the richest country in the world it's going to have to start doing what I am doing. I also support the arts. By that I mean I have set up an art cooperative. I do not produce the art, I sell it on the internet. I take a small percentage of sales, the rest goes to shipping and the artist. There's an old saying that I found true, 'You can make a lot of money on art but no one can make a living at it.'"

Noonan was scribbling in his notebook. Then he asked, "How many planes do you have in your flight service?"

"Two. One is for passengers and the other for cargo. Or wild game. I do not like to take chances with my clients."

"Good for you," Noonan said as he wrote. "How many pilots do you have on payroll?"

"Two. And unfortunately they are both my ex-husbands. We do not get along, let me add quickly. Personally, anyway. At this point it's strictly business. They are very good at what they do." She looked over her shoulder as if she was looking to see no one was in back of her. "But that's all they are good at. They are paid well when they work," she shook her head as she added, "and the rest of at time …" she let the sentence hang and raised her hands to nonverbally say, 'what else can I say.'

"How long have you been running the lodge business?"

"Thirteen years come spring."

"Both husbands …"

"*Ex*-husbands .."

"Ex-husbands have been involved with the business the whole time."

"That was a problem. Both times. Had to buy them out. Both of them."

"Are they black?"

"If I am, they are. Being black here in Micheaux is something that one *is*, not what one looks like. Kind of like the rest of America. Most people who are black you would not know it unless they told you."

"So both husbands," and Noonan quickly added, "**Ex**-husbands, have been flying for you for 13 years."

"Correct."

"When I talked with Attucks, he said there had been an organ delivery in the same vehicle as the missing diamonds."

"News to me. I knew there was going to be an organ donation. We're a small town, detective. You are a detective, aren't you?"

"Works for me. So you knew there was going to be an organ transplant. But you were never asked to fly the organ to Omaha?"

"I was never asked."

"Could your plane have made it that far?"

"Sure. My Cessna 206 could make it in one hop."

"But you were never asked."

"Correct."

"Attucks said it would cost too much to send it by plane."

"Not my plane. I would not have charged. And I only knew the kidney had gone by armored when I was told the operation was a success."

"You knew the recipient?"

"No, the donor. Like I said, detective. This is a small town."

Noonan chuckled. "Welcome to the real world. Do you mind if I look around the property?"

"Not at all." She opened a desk drawer and handed him a ring of keys. "Look wherever you want. Just leave the bags of gold behind the slaughterhouse buried and fuel the 206 if you take it up for a spin."

CHAPTER 23

"So you're that detective from out of the East?"

Aiden Remboldt caught up Noonan as the detective was touring the slaughter house. If Aiden was black there was no visual clue. But it was clear why Elizabeth had been drawn to him. He was what a Westerner would call a man's man. He was a good two inches over six feet, did not have an ounce of fat on his body and could have starred in a Marlboro advertisement. He had a healthy handshake and he put a foot up on a slaughtering beam as he pulled a tobacco tin from his jean pocket.

"Everyone in Micheaux knows you're in town. Noonan, right?"

"It'll work."

"All about the diamonds. You'll want to talk to everyone. So," he spread his arms, "here I am."

"Nice of you to be so amiable," Noonan said. "You ever work in this slaughterhouse?" Noonan swung his hands out to indicate the slaughterhouse where they were standing.

"Five years. I was half-partner in all of this," he spread his hands as if to encircle the entire now-Reynolds property. "Sill am, so to speak. We made money. Good money. Then things went south. Way south."

"That can happen," Noonan said as he pulled his notebook out. He looked up and said, "I don't want this to come as a shock to you but Attucks does not have very nice things to say about you and his mother."

Remboldt laughed. "Attucks does not have anything nice to say about anyone. He's into one thing: money for Attucks. He conned and misled Kankan for years and lined his own pocket. Nothing is enough for Attucks."

"You think he figured a way to steal the diamonds?"

"If it were possible, yes. The way I hear it, the diamonds left under guard and arrived empty. That tells me they were stolen by the armored car people. One of them has a history, you know."

"I do. Anything else I should know?"

"I don't know what you know." Remboldt smiled. "I'm just a bystander. I'm not expecting anything out of the Kankan will. Right now, I'm doing all right. I fly for Reynolds, my old company, so to speak, and make do with gypsy flying for cargo aircraft out of Sioux Falls."

Noonan pretended to look through his notebook. Remboldt was not fooled. "Hey, we're both big boys. Don't pretend you're looking for something in those pages. Ask me the questions you really want to ask. I've got nothing to hide."

"Well, since you said it so nicely, I've got a few questions."

"Shoot, Luke."

"Did you know the man who donated the kidney?"

"Old Man Harrison. Yeah, everybody does. Had a loser nephew in the pokey. Needed a kidney. Everyone told Old Man Harrison the kid wasn't worth it. But blood will tell. As soon as the kid was free, the operation took place."

"Who paid for the operation?"

"Attucks. I guess it was something Kankan wanted. He was absolutely devoted to anything family."

"Attucks or Kankan?" Noonan asked.

"Who was devoted to family, Attucks or Kankan?" Aiden was surprised at the question. Then he added, "Not Attucks, that's for sure."

"Why didn't he send the kidney by plane?"

"Easy one. He's cheap. He'd chase a penny across a crowded freeway."

"Your ex-wife says she would have done it for free."

Remboldt shook his head. "Yeah, she says that *after* the fact. There's not a lot of love lost between Attucks and his mother."

"But the kidney could have gone by plane, right? No reason to worry about air pressure affecting the organ."

"Done all the time. Gotta keep it real cold, lots of ice, and in a secure container."

Noonan looked around. "Lots of ice. But I don't see any ice here."

"Won't until its slaughtering time. Ranchers don't just show up with livestock and say, 'Here we are.' I ran this place for five years. You had to plan ahead. Ice, crates, butchers, cold storage vans to get the meat out."

"So your ex-wife could not have flown the kidney out?"

"Tough question. She could have gotten ice from somewhere in Micheaux and packed it around whatever the organ was in, yeah, she could have taken it."

"But she didn't."

"You got it. Any other questions?"

"A couple. Are you completely out of the Reynolds company?"

"Yes and no. For the company to survive I am taking my payout over years. Pay has been sketchy for years. I'm still owed money and I still fly for Reynolds. I need the money and if it goes under, I get squat."

"How about the other ex-husband?"

"Jasper? Odd man. Sexually, that is. Elizabeth left me and found him. Nude parties in Sioux Falls. Bondage and stuff like that. I was not into that. He was a long fling for her. He was a pilot. Just like me. A good one. He still flies for her. They were business partners and, like me, she bought him out over time. I'll bet she's still paying him inconsistently just like me. We don't talk much."

"He lives in Micheaux?"

"Want his address?"

CHAPTER 24

If Jasper Reynolds was black, there was no way to tell it. If he was straight, there was no way to tell it. While he might have been sexually straight, there was no way to tell that either. A gracious way to describe him, Noonan thought to himself, was unabashedly effeminate. Noonan could care less about a suspect's sexuality. If it had no bearing on a case, it is irrelevant.

"Took you long enough," lisped Reynolds. "I knew you'd be coming this way."

"Small town, eh?"

"You can say that again," and he whimpered rather than spoke.

Reynolds was of average height and weight. He was dressed perfectly including a pair of shined shoes. Considering everyone else in Micheaux Noonan had spoken with wore boots, the shoes stood out. And shined at that.

"Let me make it easy for you, copper. I don't like Attucks. He can't stand me. Elizabeth and I had a long-term fling that involved marriage and alternative sexual experiences, shall I say, in Sioux Falls, Atlanta, San Francisco and on some cruise lines. I was a business partner of hers for about six years. I still fly for Reynolds. Just like Jasper. She has not bought me out because she cannot. Probably never will. Her businesses are in the black but barely. I could have flown the kidney to Kansas City but I didn't. I wasn't asked. If I had been asked I would have got the ice from the grocery store or the ice house where you spent half an hour asking what and when Attucks bought the ice. I didn't know transportation for a kidney was needed until the diamonds were missing. I didn't take the diamonds. I don't know who took the diamonds. I do not know what is in Kankan's will but I am sure I am not listed. Is there anything I missed."

Noonan looked at his notes. "Few more items. Did you know Old Man Harrison?"

"Yup. You can talk to him if you want. He's pretty old. That's why we call him Old Man Harrison. Came here with Kankan before Kankan was Kankan. His long-term memory is good. Not so much short term. I mean he doesn't have Alzheimer's or dementia but his memory of the last few months is undependable. Was a minister. Not a holy roller or bench jumping church. Unitarian, I think. Whatever that was. Is. Anything else?"

"When was the last time you flew for Reynolds?"

"Oh, let's see, two weeks ago."

"Before or after the diamonds went missing?"

"Ha! Clever man, you are, you are. Subtle. I like that. The Reynolds planes did not fly the day before or after the diamonds disappeared. I flew two days later. And, yes, the FBI did search the plane the day the diamonds disappeared. And they searched me and my house, this one, and the plane before I flew off to the lodge. And, yes, the FBI searched the lodge. I can't think of any place they did not search. Why, I do not know. The diamonds went into the armored car. We all know that. The Muslim diamond guy, whatever his name was, verified the diamonds were in the carrying whatever before the stones went into the armored. Those stones were taken into the armored car. They left Micheaux. Period."

Noonan kind of shook his head. "A few more questions. Do you know anything about diamonds?"

"They're a girl's best friend."

Noonan chuckled. "Other than that."

"They are small, white and worth a lot of money."

"What about the other gems in the collection. The ones that were not stolen. Why would someone only steal diamonds and not all the gems?"

Jasper shook his head. "Haven't a clue. Maybe the thieves ran out of time. Maybe the other stones were not as valuable as the diamonds. Maybe the thieves had a fetish for diamonds. Why do you think only the diamonds were stolen?"

Noonan smiled as he shut his notebook. "If I knew that I would really be Sherlock Holmes."

CHAPTER 25

Noonan spent the night in Micheaux and took a tour of the city before heading back to Sioux Falls. He had seen many a small town in his life, and his career. Most were stationary in the sense nothing was going to change. Those towns were easy to recognize. They were sleepy, traffic came through but did not stop, talented people left, the rich lived uptown and the only change was the buildings getting older. If you came through a decade later, the same people would be sitting on the same benches in front of the same buildings and their grandchildren would be watching the clock creep toward their 18th birthday so they could leave to join the Army, Navy, Coast Guard, Marines and never come back.

But Micheaux had promise. Not only did it have a Post Office, it also had a UPS and FedEx stop. It had a high school and a community college. You could graduate from high school and get a good job in town. It had utility systems in place. People were making money here. Money attracts people. It attracts construction, road extension, nightclubs, boutiques, doctors, malls and everything good and bad that is the fingerprint of a community on the move. There were no park benches, only bus stop seating which emptied every hour. Kankan's vision of a prosperous city was certainly alive even though he was not.

All the way back to Sioux Falls, Noonan rolled what he knew over in his mind. Everything that had happened made sense only if there was a larger picture for the pieces to find into. He knew there was a bigger picture about to snap into focus. He was looking for what he called a 'trigger.' He had already seen one. That was the organ transplant. It was too convenient in terms of time. It was part of the diamond heist. How, he did not know yet. But what he did know was that Attucks – who he viewed as the most likely participant in any scheme – had delayed the sending of the precious stones until the transportation of the organ was required.

Further, it was clear Attucks had obscured the trail of matching the stolen diamonds to their original owner. As soon as the precious stones had been removed, Attucks had the bodies melted. That way, there was no way to match the stolen gems to the bodies of the original owners of the heirlooms. Since the stolen diamonds had not been GemPrinted, there would be no way to identify them as the stolen. Even if it could be proven that Attucks had 63 diamonds, there would be no way charge him with a crime because it could not be proven those were the stolen diamonds.

Further, even if the diamonds were found in his possession, there was no crime because there was no benefit to him. He was the executor of Kankan's will, not a recipient of any property. Or that's what Noonan had been lead to believe. So even if the diamonds were found and proven to be the stolen stones, Attucks was still in the legal clear because he could not profit from the sale of the stones.

Then there was the question as to why only diamonds were stolen. Generally speaking, a sapphire is worth half per carat when compared to a diamond. But still worth stealing. So why were just the diamonds stolen? And, of course, how were the diamonds stolen?

But there was a big something happening.

Very big.

A lot bigger than 63 diamonds.

But whatever was planned had not snapped into focus yet. There was still a trigger out there, something that was going to snap everything into focus. When that trigger was pulled, every aspect of the entire matter of the departed diamonds was going to snap into focus immediately and if he and Walrus were not prepared to work fast, the perpetrators were going to 'get away with it.'

The theft of the diamonds had been the first trigger. Had he missed something? Maybe he should rethink the theft, but from a different angle.

When he got back to his hotel room in Sioux Falls, he started the re-research process. It was still before five when he got Ambrose Brody on the phone.

"Captain! Found my diamonds yet?"

"I'm still looking. I had a few more questions for you."

"Anything I can do to help."

Noonan fiddled with his notebook. "When did you and Attucks connect to sell the precious stones?"

"I didn't connect with him. I connected with Kankan before he died. The three of us, Kankan, Attucks and me, worked on the sale of the heirlooms. It was a long process so there was not one particular moment when we connected. It was a process."

"But you did not choose Attucks, right? Kankan did that?"

"Kankan did. I only dealt with him midway through the process. He, Attucks, was to take a class to learn how to remove the gems. He would sell the metal and I would market the stones."

"How long before he finished removing the gems before he said he was ready to send the diamonds for GemPrints?"

"Oh, about six months. They were other issues he had to take care of."

"Issue with the heirlooms?"

"No. He didn't say. Kankan was dead by then so I assume it was probate kind of issues."

"When did he set the final date for the transfer of gems?"

"Oh, about a month before I examined the stones."

A gong went off in Noonan's mind.

About the same time the organ transfer was in the process of being negotiated.

"Did you set up the GemPrint delivery?"

"No. Attucks did. It was on the route of the Micheaux armored car service. He wanted to keep to the contract with locals."

"He never suggested a Sioux Falls armored car?"

"Not as far as I know."

"The first time you were in the vault, for the two days examining the stones. It was just you and Attucks?"

"Yes. Both days."

"No other security?"

"There was a guard outside but he never came in."

"Did the guard do any kind of a personal search when you went in or came out?"

"Not when I went in. Whenever I came out, like for lunch or use the restroom, he would have but Attucks waved him aside."

"When you went in the morning of the pickup, it was early, right?"

"About 5 in the a.m."

"You said the vault was cold."

"Frigid. It was for the organ."

"So you didn't stay long."

"A few minutes, that was all. I just popped open a dozen of the envelopes, looked inside and made sure there was a stone inside."

"But you never rolled any of the gems out of the envelope?"

"No. Just looked."

"When you went out, was the security guard there?"

"Yes. So were the three armored car people, two women and a man. None of them went inside the vault."

"I saw security footage of the delivery," Noonan said. "But I didn't see any footage from inside the vault."

"I don't know. I don't think there was a camera inside. That vault was from the 1930s. Probably never had an inside camera."

The gong chime in Noonan's cerebellum was now clinging loudly. After he hung up the phone, he placed a call to Walrus.

"Busy tomorrow?"

"I was going to rob Fort Knox but it's too far from Sioux Falls."

"Pick me up at 9. We're going to Micheaux to look at security footage."

"We've already done that. I've done it twice."

"Did you know Attucks went back into the vault later that night. Alone?"

"NO!"

"Yes!"
"I'll see you at nine."

CHAPTER 26

"Well," said Walrus when he pulled up the Noonan's hotel and pushed the passenger car door open. "You had some unexpected news and so do I."

"You mean the late visit to the vault?"

"First time I've heard of it."

Noonan strapped himself into the unmarked and asked, "So, what news do you have for me?"

"Bits and pieces. Not sure what they mean. But I am, we are, a lot further down the road than we were two, three days ago."

"Speak on, oh knowledgeable one!" Noonan made a motion with his hand for Walrus to continue.

"I did get a look at Kankan's will. I'm shocked the FBI let me look at it but, hey, I'll take all the help I can get."

"And what did it say?"

"Not much. It was short and sweet. What it did not say was that anything would be left to a certain individual. But it did state Attucks was the Executor and he was not to inherit any property or cash."

"Kind of says what he thought of Attucks."

"I'd say so," Walrus laughed. "I'll bet Kankan knew he had to have someone be the executor and Attucks was the only one he had."

"Well, who did he leave his land and cash to?"

"No one. He said he wanted his assets to go for the benefit of the city and Attucks was to make the distribution."

"The city of Micheaux?" Noonan shook his head. "It doesn't exist."

"At the time of Kankan's death, it was on the drawing board. He was the driving force. Then he got cancer and died. With him went the City of Micheaux. So there is no city."

Noonan shook his head slowly. "Which means Attucks can give property money to whomever he likes."

"As long as he is not the recipient."

Noonan closed on eye as he thought for a moment. "Attucks is a very clever guy. I'm sure he's ..."

Walrus cut him off. "It's already in the works. I'm not sure how it's going to come off but I've got the pieces of the future so to speak."

"Pieces of the future?"

Walrus looked sideways with a smirk. "Got one up on yah, didn't I, Bearded Holmes." He chuckled. "I checked the corporate and business records for the state. Didn't take long for something to pop."

"You are the 'Mustached Holmes,' Walrus. Tell the old man what you found."

There were no business licenses that rang bells but I found four LLCs, Limited Liability Corporations. There were not linked in any way b-u-t the names ran bells."

"Go on."

"I don't know what it is like in North Carolina, but in South Dakota you can form a LLC using paperwork on line. You do not need a lawyer."

"Sounds reasonable."

"It takes some study but you do not need a lawyer. This is particularly helpful in South Dakota because we are so small. It is said we are not a state but a small town on a very long street."

Noonan shook his head. "I've heard that before. Everyone says, 'we're a very small town.'"

"To a certain extent that is true. Again, I do not know what it is like in North Carolina but here in South Dakota we have groups. Like many small states, our political elite, social elite and business elite are all the same people. So, whatever transpires in any one of those groups is known by everyone in every one of those groups. Below them, where most of us *peons* live," he emphasized the word *peons*, "we each have our own community. I know a lot about what is going in law enforcement and the courts but not diddly in the arts or business community."

"Make sense."

"What I am working around to tell you is that what I found was hidden enough that casual research would not discover it. In other words, if Elizabeth Reynolds bought another lodge, everyone would know it because she'd have to start buying supplies for the lodge, advertise for hunters, etc. That would be public knowledge, period. Whatever she did, it would leave trails in the community, so to speak."

"And?" Noonan gave Walrus a questioning look.

"What I am saying is that what I found was hidden. Had we not discussed legal paperwork, I would not have followed that lead. Even when I did, what I found was interesting but made no sense. At least not yet."

Noonan shook his head like a character in a cartoon does to try to make sense of what the character had just heard. "Explain."

"OK. When I looked for businesses and corporations with any of the names we had, I got zip. Again, I like that term. When I pulled up owners, shareholders and representatives, I got a good dozen. Most of them were in businesses that had gone under. But four of them sounded alarm bells. Let's see if you can guess who the four were."

"I'm betting Attucks is one."

"Yup. But I'll get to him later. Try three others."

"If I were a betting man I'd say Elizabeth Reynolds, Aiden Remboldt and Jasper Reynolds."

"GOOD GUESS, my man. May I ask how you figured that out?"

"Gut feeling, I'd guess you'd say. Aiden showed up unexpectedly while I was interviewing Elizabeth Reynolds. The only way he knew to casually run into me was if Elizabeth told him I was on the property. He never said how he knew I was there. I didn't ask. When I spoke to

Jasper, he knew everything I had asked the other two. He said he knew because it was a small town."

Walrus laughed. "All of the South Dakota is a small town. I'm not from Micheaux but from what I have picked up, the three of them detest each other."

"Cash, Walrus, cash. Cash, like politics, makes strange bedfellows."

"Well, where's the cash?"

"When they are machinations, it means the cash is coming."

Walrus drove for a while thinking. Finally he said, "Let me think on this before I dive into the filing details."

"Before you go silent, how was Attucks involved?"

"I don't know yet. And I don't know for sure he is involved, it's all very touch and go. Elizabeth, Aiden and Jasper all filed LLCs. They clearly did not want anyone to know so they filed under odd names. Elizabeth filed under Tantanka. That was Sitting Bull's real name. I knew that from my South Dakota history class. Aiden filed as Zwieg LLC. Roger Carl Zwieg is a South Dakota test pilot hero. Jasper filed as Rustin LLC. It took me a while to figure that out. It was probably for Bayard Rustin, a black civil right and gay activist in the 1960s. That fits his life-style. Not using their real names was a way of avoiding initial scrutiny. But they all filed on the same day. Attucks had filed to become a trust two months earlier. He was clearly trying to stay below the radar. He filed under his old name, Jerome Remboldt. And consider this. He filed to become a trust about the same time Old Man Harrison was arranging for the removal of his kidney."

Noonan was silent for a long time. Finally he said, "You know, Walrus, you are right. Something is afoot. We are looking at quite a few pieces that just do not fit yet. They all broadcast money but there is no money there. My guess, and I am not a lawyer, is when the money comes, Elizabeth has to ante up and pay off Aiden and Jasper. They both told me she owed them money. If she gets money through the LLC, she can't be sued personally. If she drains the money out the LLC to herself personally, there is no money to sue for."

"That's the way I figured it too. Same for Aiden and Jasper. I have no idea to whom they owe money or how much. But if they get money personally, they could be sued. But if the LLC gets the money, it cannot be sued. The three of them are covering their fiscal butts."

"True," Noonan said thinking. "But Attucks filed an LLC. He can't get money because they will specifically state he is to receive no money."

"Faith, old man," Walrus said with a smile. "If there is money, people like Attucks will find a way."

Walrus gave Noonan a suggestive smile over his right shoulder.

Noonan caught the smile. "What?"

"Are you ready for the kicker?"

Noonan chuckled. "How can I say no?"

"Kankan's will allowed Attucks to give property for the good of the city."

"For a city which does not exist," Noonan said. "And will never be charted."

"You got it. Again, guess who got the land?"

"No! Not our three LLCs!"

"Yes. All on the same day. One week after they filed their LLCs. One-sixth of all property Kankan owned, intown and out of town."

"No!"

"Yes! And there's more!"

"Don't keep me in suspense."

"A week after that, all the property in the three LLCs was transferred to Attucks' LLC. I would not have known that unless I had discovered the names of the LLCs. Very, very much under the radar. And the transfer of land is free because there is no money involved. It's just paperwork."

"So Attucks owns the property."

"Now the kicker. He only owns half of all of Kankan's property. The other half is being held by the three other LLCs. My guess, they do not trust Attucks enough to give him all the land at the same time. They are holding back for some reason."

"Land is not money. It a lever for money. So there has to be money coming. That's the way of the world. There has got to be money involved," Noonan said. "I can smell it."

"Yup, 50% of Kankan's land is distributed," said Walrus and then he looked at Noonan over his right shoulder again. "So, where's the money? Those three are not going to give Attucks millions of dollars in property for free. They hate him. So, there's got to be some money involved here. The only money I can see is the settlement from the insurance company for the diamonds. But that is not something that is going to come soon. If we can prove any of them are involved in the disappearing of the diamonds, that makes the insurance money evidence of a crime and it can never be used by any of them. Right now, I do not see a dime."

"Neither do I." Noonan looked through the windshield as Micheaux appeared in the distance. "Let's not let Attucks know any of this. Let's not spoil the surprise."

"Works for me."

CHAPTER 27

As is said in many parts of America, Attucks was not a happy camper when he saw Noonan and Walrus get out of the unmarked. In fact, he was down-right rude which, in his case, was his normal *persona*. He was in his office at the bank when Noonan and Walrus arrived. His demeanor was not pleasant.

"For Jesus H. Christ sake, what are you two doing here? I've told you everything you wanted to know. Three times! Shown you everything there is to show!"

Noonan was a master at dealing with irate perpetrators. "Attucks, you have been a very bad boy. You went into the vault after the precious gems had been examined and locked into the cabinet. You didn't tell Walrus that when he was here last time."

"So," snapped Attucks. "What's the diff? The gems were in the cabinet when they left the vault. Ambrose Brody confirmed that. He confirmed that in the vault and when he talked to you."

"But the diamonds are missing, Attucks. That makes me suspicious," Walrus said softly. "Everything is on the table."

"Come on," Attucks growled. "I had a kidney that had be kept refrigerated. You knew that." He pointed a shaking finger at Noonan. "It was going to be sent out in the armored car the next morning. I got the kidney from the doctor and it had to be kept refrigerated. The armored was leaving at five in the morning to get the kidney to Omaha in time for the insertion or whatever the operation is called."

Walrus was cucumber cool. "Attucks, you didn't lie. You just didn't tell me all the truth. That makes you a very naughty boy. Sometimes naughty boys go to prison. When a crime is involved it's called conspiracy, false testimony, perjury, accessory after the fact and, who knows, maybe him accessory in the theft of 63 diamonds. You could be in prison for a long time, my friend. A *very* long time."

"Don't give that pap, copper." Attucks was irate. "I know my rights. I did not lie. I did not tell one lie. So go ahead and arrest me. Then I'll sue the living bejesus out of your department."

Noonan calmed the discussion. "Atticus, no reason to get uptight. What you did not show us was the security footage for your time in the vault when you put in the organ. You said it was only for a couple of minutes. OK, let's look at the footage. Do you have a problem with that?"

"Not a one," snapped Attucks. "Not a one. Just make it quick. I've got work to do."

"Well, why don't you just give us a copy and we'll be gone. How's that?" Walrus was smiling.

"Fine with me. I'll give it to you on a flash disk. Will that be enough to get you gone?"

"For the moment, yes," replied Walrus. "But if any other issues come up, well, you know, we will be back. And," he gave Attucks a stern look, "if we have to come back because you didn't tell us the truth, the whole truth and nothing but the truth, we'll be here with some bracelets for you."

"You don't scare me, copper," snapped Attucks. "Stand here and you can watch me get the footage." He turned to the computer on his desk and fiddled with some letters and numbers on the keyboard. Over his shoulder he snapped, "Don't try to see my password. If you want more than I am giving you, get a warrant."

"I might just do that," Walrus said slyly. "But if I believe you are covering up a crime, well, I don't need a warrant. You can sue all you want but in this state, and most of them, when you find someone *in flagrante,* you don't need a warrant and judges usually side with the police."

Attucks grumbled a lot as he pulled up frames on the computer screen and they snapped one scene into view. He turned sideways, pointed to the time and date stamp at the bottom of the screen. To Walrus specifically he said, "See that time and date stamp?"

"Yup."

"Do you see it is the day before the diamonds disappeared and is at 10:30 p.m."

"Yup."

"That's what I am giving you. On this." He pulled a flash disk from off his desk. "Will that make you happy?!"

"It will make me very happy, Attucks. But like I said, if it shows any hanky-panky, well, I will be back. And I will not be happy."

Attucks jammed the flash drive into the computer, swept his mouse to the screen and did a download. Then he handed the flash drive to Noonan. "I don't trust the locals," he said as he handed Noonan the flash disk. "Now," to Walrus. "I have given you 100% of what you wanted and 100% of what is available on this screen for the time I was in the vault. That's it. If you want more, get a warrant."

Walrus leaned toward Attucks. "I want to be very happy, Attucks. If I am not, I will be back and I will not be happy when I come back."

Attucks snarled. "**IF** you come back, come with a warrant, copper."

CHAPTER 28

Walrus drove the unmarked about a mile from the Micheaux Bank before he pulled over. He dug a laptop out of the back seat and loaded up the flash drive. He and Noonan watched carefully as Attucks was shown walking into view. The organ box was not large, about the size of a briefcase. Attucks was holding the box gingerly, a hand on the top and bottom. He walked to the door of the vault with a security guard behind him. Attucks turned his back to the guard and hunched as he punched in the numerical combination for the door. The door swung open and Attucks entered. The security guard did not.

Eighteen minutes later, Attucks came out.

Eighteen minutes!

Noonan and Walrus looked at each other with questioning faces.

Attucks did not appear to have anything with him when he came out. He exited the vault and closed the door. He punched in some numbers and then turned to the guard. He nodded and both men left the screen.

"Well," said Walrus. "What do you think?"

Noonan said nothing for a moment. Then he said, "Run it again. But when I say 'stop,' freeze it."

Walrus laughed. "Freeze. Nice touch."

Walrus started the footage again. The two men watched as Attucks walked toward the vault door.

"Freeze it."

"You got it, Chief. What do you see?"

Noonan hunched toward the screen. "Look at the way Attucks is holding the organ box. Hand on top and bottom. If you were walking with a box that size, you'd probably have your two hands under the box, not on the top and bottom."

"Yeah," Walrus replied. "Can I go on?"

"Sure."

Walrus ran it for a few more seconds then Noonan told him to stop. "There," Noonan said as he pointed at the screen. "See how Attucks has his back to the camera at the vault door. That's odd. Like he wants to hide what he is doing. Notice that he is hunching. He's hiding something. But what?"

Noonan thought for a moment and then said, "Back it up again. To where he is coming down the hallway to the vault."

Walrus backed up the footage and ran it again. When Attucks came into view, Noonan said, "Stop."

"Hand on top and bottom, humm." Walrus said. "You know what I think?"

"Same thing I think," said Noonan. "The hand on top is to hold the lid down. The lid is not secure. It could mean the organ box was not taped shut by the doctor."

"Which I doubt," added Walrus.

"Or, more likely," Noonan mused. "Attucks is taking something *into* the vault."

"Whatever it was, he didn't come out with it." Walrus scratched his head. "But he must have come out with the diamonds. Whatever it was he took in, it substituted for the diamonds."

"Maybe," Noonan said. "But we'd better make sure we have all our ducks in a row. Let's talk with the organ doctor here in Micheaux."

CHAPTER 29

"I have paid for every ticket I've ever received," snapped Dr. Hazleton Fitzsimons said when he saw Noonan back at the Micheaux clinic.

"Haven't robbed any banks lately," said Walrus with a laugh. "Actually, we're here for information, not with handcuffs."

"Ha, ha." said Fitzsimons flatly.

"Just a few simple questions about the kidney you took out of Old Man Harrison."

"I cannot confirm it was from anyone. The law protects doctors and patients."

Noonan chuckled. "Not a problem. Just some general questions. When you removed that kidney, or any kidney to keep your answers in the general, what do you do with the kidney after it is removed?"

Fitzsimons looked at Noonan suspiciously. "What was wrong with the kidney that might have been removed here?"

"Nothing as far as I know," said Noonan with a smile. "I'm just asking a general question."

"Generally," Fitzsimons said, "concerning no patient in particular, the organ is transported in a box with three plastic bags. One bag contains the organ in a medicinal solution. The bag with the organ is placed inside a larger bag with a salt solution and then the two bags, one of them immersed in the other, are put in a third bag full of saltwater. Then ice is put around the bags. After that, the box is sealed."

"How is the box sealed?" Walrus asked.

"Taped."

"Do you use a special tape. Maybe medical tape or something like that?"

"We use whatever tape that is here at the hospital. I suppose you can buy that brand of tape in a store. It's not duct tape or Scotch tape. I guess you could call it shipping tape."

"But it's not tape that you would only use in a medical procedure?"

Fitzsimons laughed. "You've been watching too many medical television programs. We use what you call surgical tape on the outside of the body, to be nonmedical about it. In answer to your question, we do not use special tape for organ boxes – and I am not saying we have had any organs removed here at the hospital."

"Of course not, doctor." Noonan cut in. "Now, after the organ is in the box. Where do you need to store the box?"

"A refrigerator is fine. The key is to keep the organ temperature stable. Not too hot and not too cold."

"How long can the organ remain viable, I guess that's the word I am looking for, if it is kept refrigerated?"

"Well, the sooner it is in the body of the recipient the better, of course. Twenty-four to thirty-six hours would be the upper limit."

Noonan thought for a moment and then said, "My wife is an Alaskan. I don't know that there are that many organ transplants up there but if an organ was removed in a village, it gets pretty cold in Alaska. If the organ was in one of those boxes and the temperature outside was really low, would that affect the organ?"

Fitzsimons gave a strange look. "Six or seven hours would be fine but not much more than that."

Noonan picked up the nuance. "Doctor, off the record, you seem to have found that question to be, shall I say, revealing. Do you know something you'd like to tell us but cannot?"

Fitzsimons was suddenly very nervous. "Actually," he said as he looked at the ceiling and then out a window onto Micheaux's main street. "It was a question which has come up, so to speak. I gave the same answer."

"I see," Noonan said. "Now, suppose, just suppose, this hospital removed a kidney. I'll assume it was during the day. Say at noon. The kidney would then be placed in this organ transplant box and then placed in a refrigerator. Would that be the normal procedure."

"Correct."

"And it would stay in your refrigerator, here at the hospital, until it was picked up by the person or company who was responsible for transporting it to the recipient."

"Correct."

"Is the hospital opened 24/7?"

"Yes, in the sense there is always someone here. But the regular staff is only here until about eight."

"If the organ box was picked up here before eight and placed in a conventional refrigerator, would that damage the organ?"

"No. It's the intense heat or cold over a long period of time, while the organ is still viable, that would cause the problem."

Walrus was on the implication like white on rice. "So, theoretically, if an organ was in an organ box in a very cold environment for, say, seven hours, it would still be viable?"

"I'd say yes. But not much longer than that." He stalled for a moment and then said, "But I never said that."

CHAPTER 30

"Well," Walrus said thoughtfully as he and Noonan headed back to Sioux Falls. "Now we know for sure Attucks is involved in the diamond theft. All we have to do now is figure out how he did it. Could he have substituted pieces of ice for the diamonds. Ambrose Brody said he did not actually roll any of the diamonds out into his hand the next morning. He just peered inside some envelopes and squeezed others. And he said it was very cold in the vault when he checked the diamonds. So he would not have detected any coldness in the envelope."

"Maybe," Noonan said thoughtfully as he looked out at the flatness of South Dakota. "If Attucks had put in small ice cubes that appeared to be diamonds, they would have melted along the way. The cabinet was airtight so when the cabinet was opened in Omaha, there would have been a flood of water. Or at least some water. No one has said there was a flood of water in the cabinet when it was opened. In Omaha. If the cabinet drawers were air-tight, when the drawer with the diamonds was opened at the GemPrint facility in Kansas City, there would have been water in the bottom of the drawer. No one said there was."

"We didn't ask," replied Walrus.

"Maybe we should have," Noonan said. "And we're still missing a few pieces of the puzzle. The FBI and your department," Noonan jerked his head toward Walrus, "did a pretty thorough search for the diamonds. I'm betting they looked in every safety deposit box in the vault, ventilation system if the vault had one, the office Atticus uses in the bank and his home, the Reynolds operation planes and lodge, everywhere. They found nothing. So maybe the point of the organ box was not to just bring something *in* but to spirit the diamonds *out*. Maybe the organ box was left open to put the diamonds inside. Then, the box was sealed and taped shut."

"Ouch," Walrus said as he shook his head. "That opens up the possibility the women and men in the back of the armored car could have slit open the box and removed the diamonds."

"Right. And it would not have had to have been a group effort either. A stop to use a bathroom was about all the time someone would need to slit out the box and pull out a bag of diamonds. Then they could have resealed the box with common tape. It might have taken, oh, 30 or 40 seconds for someone who was prepared. We didn't ask any questions about the organ box after it got to the hospital in Omaha, either. That's a lead we missed. Now that I am thinking about it," Noonan mused. "If the diamonds had been replaced by ice, could the water from the ice have drained in the armored car? Maybe the cabinet was not airtight or, more logically, a small hole was drilled in the diamond tray to drain the water away. I mean, how much water was in something as small as a diamond."

Walrus nodded excitedly and said, "And a hole could have been drilled in the bottom of the cabinet. Attucks could have done that well ahead of time. The ice only had to be stable for the quick inspection by Ambrose Brody. In an ice-cold room. Then, after the organ box left the armored car, the temperature inside the armored car back went way up. The ice melted and the water seeped out into the armored car."

"We didn't ask if there was water on the floor of the armored car."

"We'd better check that out too," Walrus said and pulled to the side of the road as he reached for his cell phone. "We've got quite a few leads to follow-up on."

"I'll take a walk and think while you talk to the hospital in Omaha. And," Noonan stalled for a moment when he put his hand on the passenger door handle. "Ask them about the tape on the organ box. Was it surgical or commercial or doubled. Was there anything unusual about it? And, of course, did anyone associated with the operation have a criminal record?"

Walrus was on the phone when Noonan leaned back inside through the open passenger side window. "And while you are making inquiries, ask about the gold and silver that was sent to the precious metals company in Sioux Falls. Anything unusual there? Was there a payment on the precious metals. Who got the money and when?"

"I can call in the questions," Walrus said.

"And the GemPrint people. Was there any water in the bottom of the diamond tray when they opened it?"

"Don't expect an answer for a few hours."

"I'm not going anywhere," Noonan said. "Tomorrow is fine. I think we should re-interview the armored car trio. We should have done that earlier."

"Shoulda, coulda, woulda," chuckled Walrus. "The story of my life."

"You are not the Lone Ranger," replied Noonan with a smile.

CHAPTER 31

Throughout the night in Sioux Falls, Noonan rolled over possibilities in his mind. In fact, not much made sense. First, it made no sense for Attucks to steal diamonds. He had shown his ability to get Kankan's property so why not use the same mechanism with the income from the diamonds. Why steal something you already own?

But, every indication was he was responsible for the diamond theft. From the planning when the diamonds were to be shipped to the packaging of the stones. His late night visit to the vault seemed to indicate he was most likely responsible for the disappearance of the stones. And what was he going to do with the money if he got it the same way he had maneuvered to get the property?

The historian in Noonan lurched toward using the land for profit. Historically, land is not money. It is a stimulus for money. As Alexander the Great's army was advancing across Persia, what is now Iran and Iraq, he gave his old and injured soldiers large tracts of land. Land that had previously been *satraps,* basically Persian counties. The *satrap* system had failed because the rulers were not locals. They were generals sent into drain the area of wealth. Alexander saw a better way – and changed the world. When he gave a large tract of land to an old soldier, there was nothing the soldier could do with it. Again, land is not money, it is a lever.

But it did not take long for the old soldier to figure out how to make money. He married a local girl, a Persian girl, who had a large family. Suddenly he had a workforce. It was a match made on Olympus – because there was no Heaven yet. The Persian family provided the man and woman power to grow the crops. The old soldier was a veteran and he was trusted by his old army quartermasters to provide quality food for the troops. Then, for the first time their recorded history, the Persians were making money.

If you have money, you want to spend it. So down the roads Alexander made as his army advanced, came merchants from Macedonia and Greece with all kinds of things you could buy. If you had money. Which the Persian workers did. And back up those roads went young Persians to become apprenticed to blacksmiths, barbers, doctors, road builders, home construction people and dock makers. Prosperity had followed in Alexander's footsteps and, to a certain extent, continued to this day.

But the key this success was more than land ownership, it was leveraging the land into profitability. Attucks now had the land. Using the same game plan, he would end up with the money to leverage the land into profitability. But, in his case, he did not need cash. His income would not go up but he would own all the land in Micheaux and over the long run, he could be a billionaire – and not have paid any income tax to get that way.

This was a great scenario, Noonan realized, with major flaws. First, the three LLCs which shuffled him the land had to be getting something in return. At the present time, it appeared that the properties Attucks picked up were free. He had not paid anything for the property. Millions of dollars' worth of property. But the three LLCs had held back some land. This meant they did not trust Attucks to come through with whatever bargain had been made with them on the sly.

Further, assuming any money from the diamonds would be parceled out the same way, why were the LLCs involved? The four – Attucks and the LLCs – did not like each other. Or at least they said they did not like each other. At this point in the game, anything was possible.

The most logical scenario was for the four of them to end up developing the property in and near Micheaux, turn the community into a city, and open the doors to businesses. They could lease land for warehouses. The could establish Micheaux as a Midwestern Silicon Valley. The four of them had the land and had the money. Why not use it that way?

But there was no indication this was going to happen.

So what was the point of washing land through LLCs?

Then there was the ongoing question of the diamonds. Why steal what you already own?

But as far as the disappearing diamonds were concerned, just before he crashed for the night, he thought he knew how the diamonds had been stolen. And it had nothing to do with ice. He'd run the idea by Walrus the next day.

Then he went to sleep.

CHAPTER 32

The next morning, at precisely 8:05 – and he knew because that was the time on the screen face of his electronic Beelzebubian instrument of communication torture – he got a call from Walrus. Before he could even break into a discussion on missing diamonds and, specifically, how he believe the diamonds had been stolen, Walrus cut him off cold.

"I have some bad news."

"Donald Trump is opening a golf course in Sioux Falls?"

His attempt at humor fell flat.

"The diamonds," Walrus said flatly, "have turned up."

"No!"

"Yes. I will pick you up in an hour."

"Why not right now?"

"I'm on my way."

CHAPTER 33

With more than five decades in the law and order business, Noonan thought he had seen it all. With the exception, of course, for the loo-loo calls that kept coming into his office. But, when it came to hard-core thefts and murders, he had seen – he thought – every twist and turn a crime, criminal and cabal could make.

Today, he mused, he was clearly in for a surprise.

He was correct.

Walrus did not say a word as he drove from Noonan's hotel to the office of Hortensia Rodrigues, agent for Rodrigues LLC of Sioux Falls. This was not surprising for a five-minute trip. It was also not surprising because Walrus was fuming. When he finally parked the car, he broke his silence and muttered, "This is going to be interesting."

vInside Rodrigues' office, Ambrose Brody was examining diamonds one at a time on a table covered with a black velvet blanket. Rodrigues did not give Noonan and Walrus so much as a verbal welcome. She simply indicated two chairs set against the wall on the far side of the room. After they sat down, Rodrigues came over and handed each of the men a signed contract. It was a copy of the contract between Kankan Musa and Brody and Sons.

The four people in the office of Rodrigues LLC of Sioux Falls were silent for almost half an hour. The entire time, Ambrose Brody was examining stone by stone. Finally he looked up. He nodded to Hortensia. She produced a sheet of paper on a clipboard. Ambrose read the document and signed it. Then he placed the diamonds in rows on the velvet blanket and rolled the blanket up. He folded the now-rolled blanket and placed it in a suitcase he pulled from beside the chair where he was sitting. He tipped the right index finger of his right hand at Hortensia, stood up and left the room.

It was only after Brody had left the room that Hortensia looked at Noonan and Walrus. Her speech was short and not sweet. "Gentlemen. You have a copy of the contract between Kankan Musa and Brody and Sons. Brody and Sons is now in possession of the diamonds in the contract. As Brody and Sons is now in possession of the diamonds in contract, there is no crime involved." She handed Walrus a document. "This is a notarized letter from Rodrigues LLC of Sioux Falls retracting the filing of a criminal report to the Sioux Falls law enforcement agencies. This matter is closed."

Walrus was fuming. "Which means Rodrigues LLC of Sioux Falls paid off the thieves to get the diamonds back. That is a foolhardy move. It only encourages them to do it again."

Hortensia did not bat an eye. She simply pointed at the document she had just handed Walrus. She said, "This is a notarized letter from Rodrigues LLC of Sioux falls retracting the filing of a criminal report to the Sioux Falls law enforcement agencies. This matter is closed. You may now leave."

Then she turned her back on the two and went back to her desk.

CHAPTER 34

Walrus and Noonan were standing in the Joe Foss Fields Airport in Sioux Falls as Noonan looked over his ticket to Virginia Beach.

"Sorry things turned out this way, Heinz." Walrus said as he shook Noonan's hand. "We were right on the lip of solving this crime. Then the crime disappeared."

"Just as they say in sport fishing, Walrus. You can't catch 'em all."

"Good quote," Walrus gave a short laugh. "I'll be in a better mood in a few days. A lot of effort for nothing."

Noonan patted Walrus on the shoulder. "Well, look at it this way. There will not be an unsolved on your record."

"Oh, goody goody." He pulled a sheet of paper out of his jacket and handed it to Noonan.

"What's this?"

"It's all those questions we wanted answered yesterday. Do you remember, about the organ box and if there were holes in the cabinet and drawers? And there were no diamonds in the organ box. Incoming organ boxes are searched carefully routinely. Then the FBI took it. I got answers but they're no good now."

Noonan took the paper and put it into the inside pocket of his jacket. "Let me guess, no holes in the cabinet or drawers and there is no way of knowing if the organ had extra tape because the organ box is long gone."

"You should be a cop, Heinz! There were no holes in the cabinet. It was airtight so any liquid inside, like water from defrosting ice diamonds, would have flooded out. The drawers didn't need any holes. They were just drawers, like file cabinet drawers. There was no water in the bottom of any drawers, diamonds or precious stones. We know that because the moment the diamonds were discovered to be missing, the diamond drawer was searched, top to bottom and in between. Same with the precious stone drawers. Do you have any idea how the diamonds disappeared?"

"Not yet."

CHAPTER 35

Now it was Noonan's turn not to be a happy camper. By the time he got back to his office in Sandersonville, the news of the crime/no crime had preceded him by two days. He was told that the Sandersonville Commissioner for Homeland Security, Edward Paul Lizzard III, was furious that Noonan had not come back with some newspaper-worthy kudos he, Edward Paul Lizzard III, could use to increase the budget for the Sandersonville office of the Homeland Security. After all, there had been a *Muslim* involved and nothing stirred the patriotic pot of newspaper editors more than a Muslim doing anything nefarious.

But, as was his habit, Lizzard found a way to transubstantiate a crime/no crime into headlines. He, along with the Sioux Falls, South Dakota, Commissioner of Homeland Security, stated they had "masterminded" the "extinction" of a "Muslim plot" to fund a "devious plan" involving a diamond theft. Working in tandem, the two commissioners had foiled the nefarious activities and all was now well. No, Lizzard had told the press, he could not reveal any details because it was all "hush-hush" but they, the newspaper reporters, could check with the Sioux Falls State Troopers for details of the crime and the Sioux Falls FBI office for details of the resolution of the nipping of the terrorist act in the bud. This was, of course, poppycock because everyone in

Sioux Falls knew of the diamond theft, and any-and-every FBI office in America had 'no comment' on speed dial.

The only loose wire, so to speak, was Sandersonville's own "Bearded Holmes" and he had been ordered to confine his comments regarding the nefarious *Muslim* diamond theft to a 'no comment' as well.

Noonan was not pleased with the outcome of the entire matter. In the law and order world, the end of a matter was a conviction. When politics or big money cut the investigation short, everyone with a badge fumed.

So Noonan was fuming.

He had nothing to show for his trip to the middle of nowhere. Everyone in the office knew Noonan was in a funk so, as the saying goes, 'when the old man is in a funk, leave him alone.'

Finally, well into the afternoon of the second day of fuming, Harriet, the bravest soul in the office and the *il Duce* of common sense, sat down on the empty chair next to Noonan's desk.

"Everyone knows you're in a funk," she said. "Wanna tell mama about it?"

"Not really. The bad guys got away with it."

"Sometimes they do."

"Tell me about it." Noonan snapped.

Then he proceeded to give her the barebones of the case. After he was finished she said, "Why would anyone steal something they already owned?"

"My guess," Noonan said. "Greed. I'm betting the long game for Attucks was to have the diamonds for himself and get the insurance money as well. He knew, and again, I'm guessing, as long as the cops concentrated on how the diamonds had disappeared he was going to succeed. The moment the cops linked the organ going into the vault, he knew the jig was up. At that moment, again, I am guessing, he called the insurance company and told it the thieves had contacted him for a deal. The standard return rate, so to speak, is 15%. Attucks would have known that from his jewelry classes. I'll bet he opened a Swiss or Bahamian account way back when. Then he told the insurance company the thieves wanted cash to that account. The insurance company paid and Attucks gave the insurance company the diamonds which he said had been left in such-and-such a place. The insurance company did not care. It had the diamonds and only paid 15% of what it would have had to pay if the diamonds were not returned."

"No harm, no foul."

"Any idea what's going to happen now?"

"Nope. Just a guess. I'm not on the case anymore, so to speak, but if I were a betting man, I'd say Attucks would carefully divvy the diamond money by thirds. He would probably give one-third of it to each of the LLCs. It's inheritance money so there is no income tax due."

"Just give them money, why?"

"So they can transfer the land they held back initially. I'll bet it was a shuffling game. The three conspirators do not trust Attucks and Attucks does not trust them. But slowly they will work a way for Attucks to end up with the land. That's his nut. He will own every building in Micheaux and be a billionaire. The others will get cash. At the end of the day, Attucks will end up with the land Kankan didn't want him to get in the first place."

"Didn't trust him, eh?"

"My bet. I'm also betting Kankan wrote the will that way because he knew what a slime Attucks was. I'm sure he believed there would be a bonafide city of Micheaux after his death. He might have even written a will that way but, you know, around men like Attucks, paperwork like that has a tendency to disappear."

"Attucks really fooled the old man, then."

"Maybe. Probably did not read his history."

"How's that?"

"Kankan Musa was a name that was pulled from history. The original Kankan was considered the richest man in the history of the world. After he died, his son and grandson pretty much ran the empire, Mali, into the ground. I don't see Attucks or the LLCs making Micheaux better. Or even into a bonafide city. But they got what they wanted. You know, the old Winston Churchill adage, 'if you want to ruin someone, give them what they want.'

"You might be right about that," Harriet said. "People who have never had money do not know how to deal with money. They cannot handle the pressure having money will bring. The minute it's known they have cash, there will be a line of people at their doorstep from dawn to 'til dusk."

"Let 'em suffer," Noonan snarled.

"Last question, oh 'Bearded Holmes,' do you know how the diamonds were actually stolen?"

"No, just a guess."

"Guess for me."

"Dry ice. That's why the vault was made so cold the morning the diamonds were loaded into the armored car. It had to be cold enough to do several things at the same time. First, to make the inspection of the false diamonds as short and perfunctory as possible Second, it had to allow the false diamonds to hold their shape long enough to be squeezed by the diamond assayer to prove something was in those envelopes. One of the LLC people has a slaughterhouse. Big refrigerators. I was there. The dry ice diamonds could have been made there."

Noonan took a breath. "My guess, Attucks brought the dry ice diamonds into the vault with the kidney. The transfer of diamonds was scheduled so he could take advantage of the excuse for keeping the vault icy. He spent his time dumping the diamonds into his pocket and putting in dry ice diamonds. He sealed the box and walked out with the diamonds. He could have hidden them anywhere. How long a dry ice diamond would stay whole I do not know. The back of the armored car was refrigerated all the way to Omaha. About 200 miles. When the cabinet was taken out of the armored car, the cabinet warmed up and the deterioration of the dry ice started. The cabinet was opened in Omaha so the rubies and sapphires could be removed from the two drawers. While the rubies and sapphires were being examined, the cabinet was left open. No one was watching the diamonds."

"And," Harriet said understandingly, "during the whole two hours, the dry ice diamonds were going to gas."

"My guess too. Even if some dry ice was left, the dry ice diamonds would have eroded to carbon dioxide on the trip to Kansas City. When the cabinet was opened in the GemPrint facility in Kansas City, there was no dry ice left. No dry ice, no diamonds. The logical explanation was the diamonds were stolen."

Harriet squinted one eye as she looked at Noonan. "Let me postulate. The stealing of the diamonds was just a distraction. If it had worked, the insurance would have paid for all the diamonds, and Attucks would have sold the stolen diamonds on the open market."

"Yup. I'm betting he would have weaned them out to the three LLCs. The diamonds did not have any GemPrints so they were undetectable. Diamonds out, money in. Then the money would flow to Attucks."

"And if one of them cheated, no more heirloom diamonds."

"Again, that's the way I figure it."

"A clever guy. So he got away with it?"

"I hope not. But I can't do anything about it. But there might be an agency that can. The IRS. There could be a charge of fraud here. I gave the details of the case to them. And there is no Statute of Limitation on fraud."

"I would not want the IRS looking in my life. They can find things I didn't know were there. That will put the conspirators at each other's throats."

Noonan pointed to his face. "Do you see the look of surprise here. By the way, when your wife asks for diamonds, what's the best gift for her?"

"Diamonds?"

"No. A deck of cards."